THE SPY DETECTOR

By Paul Jones

2022

Copyright protected.

'Then said Achish to his servants, "Lo, you see the man is mad; why then have you brought him to me? Do I lack madmen, that you have brought this fellow to play the madman in my presence?..."' 1 Samuel 21: 14-15

'When sorrows come, they come not single spies but in battalions.' – Claudius (Hamlet)

CHAPTER ONE

Theo could hardly contain his excitement. He was surely at the peak of his powers. Before him lay the greatest instrument ever devised by or for mankind. And now it was finished. He peeled off another strip of Sellotape and twisted it around the wobbly cardboard frame, just for extra security. Then he leaned back in the dining room chair and gazed at the amazing contraption on the table. His Ace Spy Detector was ready.

What was even more amazing about his machine was the simplicity of its construction. It was largely fabricated out of cardboard kitchen towel rolls, two pizza cartons, a bicycle lamp and the lens of a telescope which Theo had previously used to spy on his neighbours, in case they were working for 'the other side'. (And of course, string, of which Theo always had a plentiful supply.) These were difficult times, and you could not really trust anyone. But local security must wait for now. This was a gift to the whole nation for which he would surely be knighted. You can keep your silicon chips and lithium batteries he thought.

He gazed at his creation. It would soon be time to see if it worked. But his legs were shaking so much in the elation of success. He rummaged in the sideboard drawer and found a packet of Tunes. He had a tendency to breathe through his mouth. He did not breathe through his mouth because he was a lunatic, but because he suffered from catarrh. But the tendency did not help in people's assessment of his character. Well, actually, it did help when they interviewed him for his sick benefit. The lady at the office said it was quite obvious that he was 'not well'.

She was always most helpful, even getting up and holding the door open for him when he left. They took great care of him, often interviewing him in pairs.

The problem, as is always the case with genius inventors, was getting his unique gadget to the attention of the government. Those philistines never listened. He had worn himself to a frazzle designing and building his earthquake machine. Was there anyone else in the world who could make one out of an old bicycle and tumble drier? He had laboured day and night, hardly eating. And all for nothing. Had anyone even bothered to reply to him? It was a disgrace. Guardians of the country, were they? He would show them.

He got up from the dining table and went to his computer. On the television in the corner, the DVD was playing his favourite espionage film *Funeral in Berlin* with Michael Caine. He had a huge collection of Cold War spy movies, from which he had learned most of his tradecraft. But, much as he was fascinated with spy fiction and the like, it must wait. The nation's security was in peril. He checked his emails for replies.

He had sent one recently to the new but short-lived Prime Minister Liz Truss. Perhaps she would be more open minded than her predecessors. He had not been able to find an email address for her personally, so he had used one from a government missive about pensions. He checked the address carefully.

donotreplytothisemail@gov.uk.

Yes, that was correct. Why had they not responded? It made no sense. Of course, he knew that Number Ten was riddled with spies. Indeed, he had written to Boris Johnson to inform him. Only afterwards had he realised the folly of trusting someone with such a foreign-sounding name. Theo laughed triumphantly. The fools! They had not believed him when he told them about the myriad spies who infested the upper reaches of the British establishment. Now he could prove it! How ridiculous they would look.

He cleaned up the table. He did not want to leave any traces which might give clues as to the secrets of his amazing machine. Then he opened the curtains, picked up the phone and ordered another pizza. It was still light. In a while, he would go out and test his amazing invention. First, he had to eat. And then later he must begin the hard work of promoting the fruits of his brilliance.

An hour later, the pizza man arrived. As usual, he knocked on the door, left the pizza in the porch and then ran back to his car. *What did he have to hide?* thought Theo. And then, when it was too late, he realised the pizza delivery boy could have been his first opportunity to test the machine. He damned himself for his inattention. It would have meant that he did not have to go out, something he tried to avoid. Theo was a creature of the dark and the indoors. More at home with the curtains drawn and the door bolted.

He made his way to the kitchen, stepping over piles of books spread all over the floor. The chaos of the house and the diversity of the titles both testified to his erratic genius: *Crop Rotation for Beginners*, *The Life of Captain Beefheart*, *The Development of Belgian Cheese in the Eighteenth Century*, *Some Common Horse Diseases*, *Chair-making in Hemel Hempstead in the Fifties*, *The Grand Chessboard by Zbigniew*

Brzezinski, Living with Chimps, The History of the CIA, You and Your Rupture, The Spy who Came in from the Cold, Raise your own Chickens, Cybernetics Made Easy, You Too Can Dance the Tango!, Hungarian in Ten Days, The Origins of Underwear, War and Peace and *I Conquered Haemorrhoids*. And many, many others. The books were all over the floor, falling off shelves, falling to bits, spilling out of boxes and getting in the way of everything he had to do. What kind of a brilliant mind could accommodate all this information? He tapped his temple in answer. Only his. For years, like so many of the great minds of history, he had lived in obscurity, waiting for the moment when all the various curves of his creative genius came to one magnificent confluence. Waiting for the time when the world, in its desperation, called on him for its salvation.

He had to go back into the dining room and sit down again. It was all too much to bear. How heavily greatness can weigh upon the mortal frame, he thought. He considered that a good phrase and went to note it down in one of his notebooks, but he couldn't find them. He rummaged everywhere. And once he had found them, he had forgotten what he wanted them for. So many things to remember, so many things to carry in his mind. But one day...

He decided to forgo a plate. He ate the pizza from the carton. That carton might be useful in the future for another of his inventions. His mother would not have approved. *Gentlemen eat from plates*, she would have said. But she was long gone. Fate had decreed that she would leave him her money and house so that he would have the independence to pursue his vital studies and research. It was all preordained. He had a destiny.

After the feast of ham and mushroom with extra cheese, he felt ready to face the world. He donned his special raincoat with secret and spacious pockets for the various gadgets he had invented. Then he picked up the Tesco shopping bag containing the Ace Spy Detector. He unbolted and opened the front door and peeped out. There were only a few people in the street. He decided to follow an old lady who worked at the local Birds cake shop. She was called Mrs…oh, what was her name. It was so very strange that a man with a photographic memory had such trouble remembering so many things. (He had plenty of books about psychology back at home and made a mental note to look it up when he returned. Clearly, there was a scientific explanation for it.) He began to trail her at a safe distance using the techniques he had learned from all his spy books and films.

As the portly old lady waddled up the street, he surreptitiously reached into his bag and pulled out the detector. He pointed it at her and pressed the trigger. But the light did not come on. Well, that was hardly a surprise. She was not a spy. Who would have thought she would be? He carried on behind her for a while, until she turned round and saw him. He smiled at her, but she seemed to have remembered something important as she had to run off. So far, so good. But it was not very far. The experiment was of no use until he identified a spy. But the night was young.

Crossing the road and walking down the main high street of the town, he could see the lights of all the shops. More people were milling about.

There was a woman from the Balkans in a sleeveless bodywarmer and flowery flowing dress, selling *The Big Issue*. She was a more likely prospect. He aimed the device at her and pressed the trigger. Again, a negative. That was more surprising. But he wouldn't know if it was a fault until he met someone whom he knew for certain was a spy.

At the end of the High Street was a pub called the Grey Man. People would be coming in and out of there on a regular basis. The problem was that it didn't look like a venue for espionage. Of course, you could never tell. That was the whole point of the spying game: you had to have credible cover. He went round the back where the car park was. Behind all the cars were some bushes where he could secrete himself. It was a little chilly, but he was wearing the thermal underwear he had bought from a survivalist site on the internet. Hiding in bushes was a dangerous thing to do as he had been arrested for something similar a few years earlier. However, the police had seen the funny side of it and let him go. (No doubt, once they had made enquiries and found that he was in touch with the government, they had decided that he was too hot to handle.) He snuggled down inside the bushes and waited. As the patrons came and went, he aimed his spy detector at them. Most of them were negative, but that was to be expected, wasn't it? After all, this wasn't Checkpoint Charlie.

A large suburban truck arrived and a man and a woman got out. Theo crouched down in his hiding place and prepared to test the detector again. They had parked very near to him, but it was getting dark. They must not know he was there, otherwise the game would be up.

'Evening Theo,' said the man. 'You taken up gardening now?'

'I hope it is gardening he's doing in there,' said his wife.

'Fertilising the plants, eh, Theo?' said the man. They both laughed and went into the pub. Damn. Now they would tell everyone he was there. He had to move on. His cover had been blown. And once your cover has been blown, you are useless as an agent. He picked himself up and dusted himself off, as recommended by Fred Astaire. Then he turned back into the High Street. But he was not downhearted. He had managed to test the man and woman and they were not spies.

Theo was out for quite a while. When he returned, it was very late. He let himself in very slowly, just in case. You can never be too careful. But there was no-one waiting for him. He entered the hall and took off his coat. He opened the cupboard under the stairs and placed the spy detector inside. Then he put the hoover up against the door and draped some ornamental Swiss cow bells over it. That would give any intruders something to think about. If anyone broke in and stole the fabulous device, he would be able to hear them. Theo thought of everything. There was no intellect in the world that was a match for his.

The outing had been a great success, although he was a bit disappointed that the light had come on when he had pointed it at next door's labrador. Clearly, some adjustments needed to be made. It had also, admittedly, been a tad embarrassing when he had pointed it at himself and the result had also been positive, but that was all to the good. He knew he wasn't a spy so that was…what was it called? A control sample, that was it. But basically, it had been a marvellous success.

After making some cocoa, he sat at the computer and began to compose an email.

Dear Prime Minister Sunak,

You may remember that I wrote to you – or rather to your esteemed predecessors - a few months ago regarding my Earthquake Machine. I know you are all very busy down there at Number Ten and have had a lot to do recently. Needs must when the devil drives and all that, eh?

Theo paused. He wanted to keep his emails short. He had read somewhere that endless emails were the sign of a crank. He did not wish to be mistaken for one of those.

However, that device is currently under review. I wish to draw your attention to the fact that my latest invention, the Ace Spy Detector, is ready and at the disposal of your security agencies. Please be assured that I want no payment for myself. The knowledge that I have served Her Majesty…

He paused again. Her Majesty? Something was wrong there but he couldn't remember what it was. Perhaps, his psychology books would shed some light on the deficiencies of his capacity for total recall, but sadly, he had forgotten about his earlier concerns.

The knowledge that I have served my country is enough. Needless to say, I cannot discuss anything in an email. Please contact me at your earliest convenience and I shall reveal all. I am at home most days, except Thursday when I go to the Benefits Office and do some shopping on the way back. (I must remember to get some more All Bran. It is on

9

offer at the Sudbury Town Co-op and if you eat All-Bran I would advise you to hurry as the offer is only for this week.) Of course, I have a mobile phone, but I am sure that you would not wish me to discuss these things in public.

PS – I must ask that you contact me personally yourself, as only then will I know that I am not the victim of a scam – which, as you may have been told by Mr Johnson or Mrs Truss, is what happened to me over my corrective shoe containing gun and communications device.

Assuring you of my best services at all times, I remain yours very sincerely…

Was it faithfully or sincerely? He was a stickler for form. But then again, people were more informal these days, especially in government.

Hoping to hear from you soon,

Theodore Ziegen-Wirbelsaule

That would do for now, he thought. No need to labour the issue or to give too much away for now.

He sent off the email to the same address, feeling confident that he would receive a reply this time. After all, one or two such communications might give the impression that he was just another crazy person. But this time, they would be sure that he was serious.

And then he noticed something. He had another email. No! Two emails! And both replies to his approaches to the Daily Globe! The Globe was a middlebrow paper with a handsome circulation. Someone had replied to him! This was promising indeed! With trembling fingers, he opened the first communication.

Hello Theo,

Thanks for getting in touch with me about your new machine. However, you should be aware that I am the fashion correspondent here. Your best bet is to contact my colleague Kevin on the Dangerous New Inventions Desk. You can find his email address at the bottom.

Best wishes,

Rumana Hamid

Home and Fashion.

Well, this was progress! Of course, he had already contacted Kevin Tregennis. In fact, he had emailed everyone on the paper. And if Theo was not mistaken, then next email was from Tregennis himself. Now at last he was getting somewhere!

Hello Mr Ziegen-Wirbelsaule – I hope I've spelled that correctly – and thank you for your communication regarding your Earthquake Machine.

I used to work the crime beat many years ago, but I'm afraid I am stuck here on the literary and arts section, so I am not sure that I am able to assist you.

Your comments were very interesting. However, I have had a word with my colleague Sarah Markstein over on the international desk – you really ought to contact her; please find her email address below - and she is convinced that the Soviet Bloc no longer exists and that while the

Russians are problem in many ways, the threat of communism has lessened significantly in the past few decades. (Which is a great relief for all of us, let me tell you.) She also said something about the KGB no longer existing – and that can only be good news, can't it?

I take your point that we can't be too careful these days – I could tell you some stories! – but to tell you the truth, although I am not an expert in these matters, I would say the best thing to do with your wonderful invention is to keep it quiet. After all, as you say, if it fell into the wrong hands…well, it doesn't bear thinking about, does it? I had a letter the other day from someone in Croydon who'd developed a cobalt bomb. (They always come from Croydon, don't they?) I told him to dismantle it pretty sharpish or I'd call the police. He saw my point of view. He's now retired to a convent for a period of reflection and re-evaluation. He is, however, working on a cure for hernias – which I am sure you will agree, is a much better use of his talents. We must all learn from each other in this life, don't you agree?

Good heavens, thought Theo. He does ramble on. He wondered if he might be some kind of crank. But no, he couldn't be. The Daily Globe would not hire people like that. He seemed like a very nice chap. Very open. Now he had two contacts and a name he had never heard of. He copied and pasted his original letter into a new email and sent it to Sarah Markstein. Things were really starting to roll.

Although he was normally a very active person – hyperactive, they said at the doctor's – Theo allowed himself to have a lie-in the next day. And why not? It was a day of triumph. By the time he was up and about, it was nearly ten.

Downstairs he had his last helping of All-Bran and then moved into the sitting room, nearly tripping over a book entitled *Organise Your Life!* which was lying by the doorway. He picked up his mail from the porch, including this month's copy of *UFO Weekly*.

No sceptic can doubt this photographic evidence! screamed the headline over the cover photo taken through the cockpit of a passenger jet. A big white arrow had been added which pointed to an almost invisible dot in the sky. Theo nodded appreciatively. He was convinced, all right. But he always had been. Good grief, hadn't he been kidnapped by a UFO? Or was that someone else? Perhaps he had a book about it somewhere. It was one or the other. Definitely.

He went to the computer and checked his emails. Someone from Nigeria wanted him to share in $16m worth of oil money which had been left in an escrow account. That might be interesting. He could use his part of the money to fund his researches. It was amazing how Destiny looked after him. Another email asked if he was ready for the coming digital meltdown. (Indeed he was: he had a cellar full of dried fruit, spam, tinned fish, face wipes, rice and teabags plus survival tent and thermal underwear, not to mention plenty to read.) But there was a third email too. And yes... it was another success! A response from the Globe again!

Hello Mr Ziegen-Wirbelsaule,

Many thanks for contacting me about your machine. I am afraid that I work on the international desk and cannot be of much help to you. We used to have a Dangerous Devices and Inventions Desk, but it proved to be a security risk, so its activities were subsumed under the Sports Desk rubric. Please feel free to contact my colleague Rob Thomas whose email you will find below.

Thanks again for contacting us,
Sarah Markstein
International Desk

Another referral! The people at this newspaper were so helpful. It was time to set up a meeting.

CHAPTER TWO

The Daily Globe had been the last of the great British newspapers to leave Fleet Street for Docklands in the eighties. The paper occupied four storeys of a big glittering building with blue glass windows. In the sunshine, the reflecting surface sparkled beautifully like the sea, although the edifice generally resembled an implement that might be used by a giant horse doctor. It had been designed by someone involved in architecture, once a respected profession, now evidence of severe anti-social psychopathology.

Kevin Tregennis and his friend and colleague, Rumana Hamid, with whom he shared a double desk, were outside having a smokers' break. Rumana didn't actually smoke but she always went with Kevin to drink her latte. Firstly, because she didn't see why smokers should get an extra break that non-smokers didn't. And secondly, because it was a good place to get office scuttlebutt. As usual, Kevin was amusing her by reading out news stories.

'There's been another Elvis sighting. But the government says it was a weather balloon.'

'What else?'

The pound has fallen again. It's expected to achieve parity with the Albanian luncheon voucher by the end of the week.'

'Do they have luncheon vouchers in Albania?'

'I don't know. I'm not even sure if they have lunch.'

'Does it say anything about Manchester United?'

'No. Still no trace of them. But don't worry, I'm sure they'll turn up. The main thing is not to give up hope.'

She nodded as if she were impressed with his wisdom.

'Anything else?'

'Yes, the Christmas pantomime at the Hackney Empire this year is Parent Goose. That's not a joke, by the way. That one is true.'

They were both chatting away like this when a taxi pulled up across the road. A very strange looking man with a goatee beard got out of the taxi. He was holding a plastic bag containing something which looked suspicious. There was a vociferous argument with the driver who had been given the exact cost of the ride and no more. Rumana had a sudden instinct. She looked troubled.

'That's Theo,' she said. 'I'm sure it is.'

'What, that bloke who keeps emailing us about espionage? The one who thinks the Cold War is still going on?'

'Yes, it is. I'm sure I've seen him before in reception. He keeps trying to tell us about his weird inventions.'

Kevin squinted at the man. He was fifty now and his eyesight was declining.

'For an anti-communist agent, he looks a hell of a lot like Trotsky,' he said.

'Perhaps it's his cover. Maybe he's a double agent,' she said thoughtfully as she googled 'Trotsky'. Theo caught their glances and beamed at them.

'Oh no,' said Kevin. But Rumana was much younger than Kevin and her reactions were slicker. With one darting move, she had her mobile phone to her ear with the speed of a gun slinger, ready to pretend to be talking to someone.

'Does he contact you as well?' asked Kevin.

'Yes, I gave him your email address. I said you looked after that sort of thing.'

'Thanks a lot. I gave him Sarah Markstein's.'

'That was daring. She'll hunt you down and kill you for that.'

But there was no time for any more talking. Theo, almost getting hit by a bus – driver under instruction - as he crossed the road, had reached Kevin and pointed to his ID badge.

'Mr Tregennis, I see? My name is…but perhaps it would be better if I didn't give you my name.'

'It's Theo, isn't it? I can't remember your surname. It's something German, isn't it?'

Theo pulled a battered business card from his pocket and handed it to Kevin. Kevin's eyes appealed to Rumana but she was having a pretend conversation with someone called Reg.

'Yes, I sent the copies over, Reg.'

'Who the hell is Reg?' asked Kevin.

'I wonder if perhaps we could have a confidential chat about something,' said Theo. Kevin looked at the card.

Theo Ziegen-Wirbelsaule.

Inventor, activist, analyst.

Anti-communist

Import-export

Lifestyle advisor

Call 0757 014 9200

theozw@u2productions.com

'Analyst? What do you analyse?'

'Well, I can see you two are getting along fine so I'd better get back upstairs and talk to Reg,' said Rumana.

'There is no Reg,' said Kevin pointedly as she left.

Theo reached into his bag and produced his spy detector. Some of the Sellotape had come off. The bicycle lamp fell off and hit the road.

'It's about this device I have invented,' continued Theo.

'Good grief, man! Don't take it out in public. They may be watching.'

Theo, realising this was excellent advice, crammed the device hurriedly back into the bag. Then he picked up the bicycle lamp and stuffed it in to his already bulging pockets. Kevin wondered if he was dangerous. He didn't look dangerous, he decided.

'You're right, of course. It's just that…nobody will listen to me.'

'Well, that's good, isn't it, Theo? It means they won't be bugging your house.'

'Ha! That shows how much you know… but I must get someone to listen to me. Someone who can help me promote my devices. Your paper is the only place where I've ever had positive feedback.'

'Well, that's the kind of paper we are, Theo. The Globe is a great paper with an eye at every window and an ear at every door. To listen is to learn and all that stuff. Now look…'

Kevin glanced at his watch.

'I've got an important meeting in a moment…'

He looked from side to side to see if anyone was watching.

'... It's about radiation weapons. I shouldn't really tell you this, Theo, but they may be sending me on an important mission, so you won't be able to contact me for a while. I'll be going ... *over there.*'

'Oh, I see,' said Theo, nodding appreciatively, adding, 'You shouldn't smoke you know. A man of your age. And you're overweight. I've got this book at home called *Your Midlife Crisis Could be a Turning Point.* I'll lend it to you. He's the same man who wrote *Irritable Bowel Syndrome Can be Your Hidden Strength.*'

'Yes, I think I've come across that. It sounds fascinating, and we will talk soon but I really have to go.'

'But you will call me. You have my number.'

Kevin clapped the strange man on the shoulder.

'Theo, you can depend on me. I think there is a really good story here. Of course, I only deal with the literary section,' he said, winking.

Theo nodded gravely. He knew all about cover. The literary section! That was very good.

Kevin shook his hand and wandered back into the building.

'Was that Theo?' said Mandy the receptionist.

'Yes. If he calls again, he needs to speak to Rumana.'

And with that he took the lift up to the fifth floor.

The Globe was like any other newspaper office. They are all open plan these days. They are quieter places too. The great print rollers and clacking typewriters of yore are gone. Only the soft tap-tapping of laptops, the gurgling of faulty latte machines and the occasional screams from the temperamental neurotics on the features pages pierce the meditative calm of the modern news organization. They are even quieter now thanks to the post Covid rush to work from home. Only a third of the staff could be seen on any particular day. Here and there, were little rooms and pods where a variety of secret activities were carried out and passed off as meetings or professional development seminars.

Suspended ceilings with sophisticated lighting systems guaranteed to create macular degeneration or blindness in the longer serving staff members flickered above. A window cleaning chariot was winched up and the operatives gazed in at the office conditions, feeling happier in their work.

When Kevin got back to his desk, Rumana was busily typing away at the desk next to him. She was buried under her mountain of wild, luxurious black hair. It was controlled only by the fact that she was able to sit on it. Kevin sighed wistfully. He had never seen so much hair on such a tiny human being. He wanted to run his fingers through it. He wanted to kiss it…he wanted to…he pulled himself together. She was half his age. She was also half his weight.

There was a post-it note from Sarah Markstein on his laptop saying, *Enjoy your last day of breathing, Tregennis. You have outstayed your welcome on earth.*

It was made even more deadly by having two kisses under it.

'Did she look angry?' he asked Rumana.

'She always looks angry. What did your friend have to say?'

'Nothing much. He's invented another device. You were a big help. It would serve you right if you *did* have to talk to someone called Reg.'

'You seemed to be getting on so well. I think you have a lot in common. That same faraway look in your eyes.'

She smiled her angelic smile at him and he forgave her in advance for anything she might ever do to him. He looked over to the large glass-fronted meeting room across the large open-plan office.

'Are the big wigs having a meeting?'

'Yes. Why do you think I'm looking busy?'

'What are you actually doing?'

'A job application.'

Kevin stared hard at the meeting room as if he would learn what was going on by concentrating.

'Redundancies do you think?' he said eventually.

'Maybe. They reckon they're going to get rid of anyone who stands about staring at management all day.'

Kevin sat down, opened his laptop and started to look busy. Rob Thomas, the huge ex-rugby player from the sports page was striding across the room looking apoplectic.

'Where's Markstein?' he asked, before disappearing into the corridor. He would keep her busy for a while.

'He looks angry too.'

'He won't bother Sarah. She's about the same size as he is.'

This was true. Sarah was invulnerable.

Kevin looked again through the windows and realised, unsettlingly, that all the managers were looking at him.

'They're looking at me.'

'Then smile and do something. Look as if you're happy in your work.'

'Oh, but I am, I am.'

He started typing something. Then he looked up and grinned like a man who loved the company he worked for. Inside the big meeting bubble, the editor Geoffrey Amis was looking at Kevin.

'Is that him?' said Jeanine Le Jean, the Financial Director. Le Jean had once been beautiful, but all the people who remembered it were dead and there had been few photos in those days.

'That's him. Kevin Tregennis,' said Amis, shaking out a couple of ulcer tablets into his palm and then irritably throwing them into his mouth, as though Tregennis had given him his ailment. They watched Kevin fumbling about in his desk drawer, pulling out all the contents on the desk. An almost hourly ritual.

'He's probably looking for a typewriter ribbon,' said Amis.

'Or a bottle of ink,' said Le Jean.

A third voice piped up. It was a sinister sounding voice. A voice without mercy from the shadows.

'Send him,' said the third voice.

'Yes, send him,' said Le Jean, like the tolling of a bell.

A consensus was achieved.

'Yes,' said Amis, nodding gravely. 'I will send Tregennis.'

They stood there, staring impassively at Kevin, like three disembodied faces in a Samuel Beckett play.

Kevin was engrossed in a task so urgent and intense that he did not notice Amis standing over him.

'Oh, hello Geoff. Sorry, I was miles away. Got to get this finished for the deadline.'

Kevin beamed with enthusiasm and inner tranquillity. He loved Big Brother.

'Busy, Kevin?'

'Oh, I'll say. It's all go, you know.'

'Yes, I'm sure,' replied the editor, trying to sound urbane. 'A moment of your valuable time, please young man.'

He waved his palm towards one of the tinier little meeting pods.

'Young man?' said Kevin. 'It's been a while since anyone's called me that.'

They both gave the smallest of laughs.

It's been a while since a lot of things happened around your desk, thought Amis, but he didn't say so. He wanted Kevin mellow. Amis smiled at Rumana, but she hardly noticed him. Rumana was very busy. She was so busy she didn't even know they were there.

Kevin rose and followed Amis into the small meeting space. It was a bit of a squeeze for both of them. They sat down. Amis closed the little door, put his coffee on the desk and then looked at Kevin for a few seconds.

Meanwhile, Rumana was aware of a huge shadow looming over her desk. She got the impression that the birds had stopped singing.

'Where is he?' said Sarah Markstein, dazzling as an exploding nova in a plangent party-pink skirt suit. She had a headband of the same colour in her night black hair.

'Erm…I think he ran away,' said Rumana with courageous flippancy. 'He said something about going to Southampton and being a cabin boy.'

Sarah nodded ominously and said,

'And well he might run away.'

She gave Rumana an 'I'll-deal-with-you-later' glare and thundered off.

In the little meeting pod, Amis finally broke the silence.

'Kevin, my old buddy. How are you? It's been too long since we had a chinwag. My fault. I've been busy but you should never be too busy for your staff. After all, they're what makes the wheels go round. How are you?'

'Er…great thanks. You know. Bobbing and weaving, ducking and diving and all that.'

Kevin laughed weakly as he said it. He felt perspiration on his brow.

'Yes…good…erm…good.'

There was a pause.

'Are you going to sack me?'

'Sack you!! Good heavens above man, no!'

Amis seemed to be glad that Kevin had brought up the subject.

'Why, have you been worrying about that? My goodness me! Of course not! I mean, honestly Kev…if I can call you Kev…why on earth would I sack you? I mean apart from anything, we're mates, aren't we?'

He made a clumsy attempt to give Kevin a matey-punch on the shoulder, but there was not enough room in the pod and he knocked over his coffee.

Mates? thought Kevin. That was news to him. Now he was frightened. He couldn't imagine Amis having any mates. He couldn't imagine Amis having any enemies either, for that matter. Amis was a shell. A whiteboard on which corporate ideology was written with a squeaky marker pen that was running out of ink. There was another pause as

Amis tried to choose his words carefully. This was a big challenge for someone who had worked in tabloids for twenty years. Eventually, he settled upon the right approach.

'How well travelled are you, Kevin? I mean…you look like a…citizen of the world, if I may say so.'

Kevin was surprised by the question.

'Well, you know…I know France and Germany well. I speak both languages fluently.'

'Good, good! Languages. First class. You know, I'm often appalled at how insular the British are, especially when it comes to learning foreign tongues. I bet you're the only person in this office with another language.'

'No, not at all,' said Kevin, seizing any opportunity. 'Rumana speaks Urdu and Sarah speaks modern Israeli Hebrew. I understand she's able to communicate with Americans as well. But that's just a rumour.'

Amis nodded thoughtfully.

'I'm ashamed that I didn't know that, Kevin. Thanks for the feedback. I should know my staff better.'

'Yes, I agree. I mean, yes, we should all take an interest in erm…each other…you know.'

'Course we should, mate. You and I…'

Amis looked around conspiratorially at the much younger people working in the office. No-one else seemed to be pretending to work. They were all chatting.

'You and I are of the same mould, Kev. We understand each other. We go back to the good days. The serious days.'

Kevin nodded but looked perplexed. He couldn't remember any good old days. And Amis was only about thirty-five to forty. He wasn't really in Kevin's age group. He understood nothing so far. He was beginning to wonder if he had ever understood anything. But he was very suspicious.

'Now, let's get down to it,' said Amis, getting down to it. 'You may have read about this conference in Kazakhstan in a few days.'

'Kazakhstan!?' shouted Kevin, unable to control his blind panic. He had been right to be suspicious.

'Calm down, man, calm down. It's not the other side of the world.'

'Yes it is. It's exactly the other side of the world. Well, nearly.'

Amis had no idea really where it was on the map, but he said,

'I meant metaphorically. Geographically…yes, it's bloody miles away. Obviously, I knew that. But anyway…now it's this new United Nations conference…er…what's it called?… *New Horizons for Humanity*. Perhaps you've read about it.'

'No. I know nothing about it. Why would I? Who cares what those crackpots, parasites and hypocrites get up to?'

'Now let's not be a cynic, Kevin. They all mean well, I'm sure of that.'

'You're not thinking of sending me, are you?' said Kevin, in utter terror.

'And why not? You're perfect for the role. I couldn't think of a better man. And what with your languages…'

'Languages? I speak French and German. What use is that in Kazakhstan?'

Amis waved this away.

'No need to worry about that. Everyone speaks English these days.'

'Well, if everyone speaks English, what use are my languages?'

'Oh, there'll be French people there. And Germans too, I should think. You'll get along famously.'

'They all speak Russian in Kazakhstan,' said Kevin, but he could have shot himself for saying it.

'Wow! Is that a fact? I didn't know you were so well informed about the place. I'm impressed, Kev. I can see I've chosen the right man. Once you get a few words of Russian together... I read that the Russians love it when someone speaks just a few words of their language.'

'They're not Russian; they just speak it. And in case you've forgotten, my job is literary editor.'

'Another excellent qualification, as far as I'm concerned. These are sensitive people...you know...humanities graduates and stuff. They've all written...erm...books...books and stuff...yeah, I'm sure they have. You'll have a lot in common with them. Lots to discuss.'

'Yeah, I know,' said Kevin cynically.

'Just get the Kruddas Prize shortlist sorted and you're good to go.'

Amis tried to think of a way to close the conversation while Kevin desperately tried to think of ways to keep it open.

'You're trying to get rid of me.'

'Oh, Kevin, Kevin. I'm wounded. I deserve better than that. Why, this is going to be a real feather in your cap.'

They both paused and looked out of the pod window where Sarah Markstein was pointing her finger at Kevin as though it were a dagger. She could make pink look dangerous. She mouthed the words, 'You're dead'.

Then suddenly, Kevin had a transformational brainwave.

'Don't you think that I'd be a little out of my depth here?'

Amis frowned. He suspected something but he didn't know what.

'Don't you think this is a job for the expertise of someone like Sarah? I mean, she is the international doyenne.'

He waved his hand at Sarah, who was sitting on an unoccupied desk, waiting to pounce on Kevin when he emerged. Amis cleared his throat. This would take delicate handling.

'Ermm...I like where you're coming from, Kevin. Humility is a virtue.'

Kevin knew he would be too terrified to tell Sarah to go, so he suggested that they ask her together. Amis shook his head.

'No, we need her here. She virtually runs the place when I'm not here.'

They looked again. Sarah had realised that something was being stirred up and had disappeared. Kevin had another idea.

'What about my wife? Could I take her with me?'

'Oh no,' said Amis quickly. 'I don't think I could swing that.'

'Why not?'

Kevin thought of Fiona. He didn't really want her with him and she wouldn't want to go. She hated travelling - but he didn't trust her enough to leave her behind. And Amis seemed very keen for him not to take her. Oh, good grief...he was already talking as if he were going.

'First class hotel,' Amis was saying. 'Expenses and all that. Everything laid on. How can you not love it?'

'Really?' said Kevin weakly.

'These people do themselves proud, you know.'

'Yes, I know that. It's the world's greatest gravy train.'

'Well, then, there you are then, matey-boy. Get stuck into the trough, old son. Gourmet cuisine, free bar...'

'I don't drink anymore.'

'Ah yes, yes,' said Amis, as if he knew this was a sore subject. 'Well, you're not on a diet, are you?'

'No, but I should be.'

They both laughed again as if they didn't really want to. Kevin looked longingly across the room to where Rumana was sitting. Sometimes in his more foolish moments he imagined that...No, he replaced his wicked thoughts with an innocent dream of running about with her in slow motion on the beach. It would have to be slow motion: he would have a heart attack otherwise... But that was a foolish dream too.

'So, can we say that's settled, Kevin?'

He wasn't Kev anymore. In any case, he had not kept his eye on the ball and Amis had won.

'Whose idea was this anyway?'

'What, the conference? Well, it's paid for – hosted I mean - by the UN, but it was organised by North Korea and Iran...'

'North Korea and Iran!? New horizons for humanity? You are bloody kidding me?'

Kevin vowed that he would never again boast that nothing surprised him.

'Well, I suppose it's their only excuse to eat properly.'

'Anyway, I didn't mean that. I meant, why, are we taking an interest in something so dumb?'

Amis leaned back, putting his fingers together like an Oxford philosophy don. There was no room to lean back and he bumped his head on the window.

'Ah yes,' he said, rubbing his head. 'Politics, Kevin, politics. Wheels within wheels and all that. It's all very complicated...you see...'

Then Amis suddenly leaned forward as if he wished to impart secrets.

'As you know, our paper was recently taken over by the big tech platform TekKnow. Well, they're a very young, go-ahead outfit. Dynamic and forward thinking and...'

'...full of it.'

'Now there you go, being cynical again, Kevin. Our new masters like a positive attitude. They're all for these new initiatives. Third World voices and all that. And if *they* like it and I tell them that *you* volunteered...' - he pointed a decisive finger at Kevin – 'well, they'll like *you*, won't they Kevin? And they'll want to keep such a forward thinking, progressive guy in a job. And it would never occur to them to think that you'd outlived your usefulness on the paper, or that you belonged to another age, an age of hot metal presses and ink pads...do you see where I'm coming from, my old mucker?'

This last was said tightly, almost through gritted teeth.

'I suppose so,' Kevin said; but he wanted to cry. There was no point in saying that hot presses and quills were way before his time and that he was fifty not eighty. He had lost and he had to accept gracefully, unless he could think of some devilish and underhand way to get out of it.

'Brilliant. All settled,' said Amis, banging the desk with the flat of his hand and upsetting his coffee cup again. Then he rose uncertainly from his comfy chair. He looked at his watch.

'Must go. I have an appointment.'

They shook hands. There was no walking this back for Kevin now. It was either Kazakhstan or wind up being scrapie and mange correspondent for the Shetland Examiner.

CHAPTER THREE

Kevin wandered forlornly back to his desk. Rumana was taking a rest from her busy job application schedule. He sat down and watched her for a while until she realised he was watching her.

'Why do you want to leave?' he asked sadly.

'Well, I want to get on, don't I? I'm only twenty-nine. I want to work on a fashion magazine.'

'You're the only thing that keeps me here.'

She turned fully to him.

'Well, why don't you get a better job?'

'There are no better jobs for me. I'm too old, too fat and too bald. I'm a clapped out time-server. I look in the mirror sometimes and *hope* that I look like Clive James. Do you know what that does to a man's sense of esteem?'

Rumana had never heard of Clive James, so she said,

'Oh, Kevin, don't be so silly. You're only fifty. You could do lots of things.'

'Oh, yes, the world is my oyster. I may book an appointment this afternoon with the careers' advisory teacher. I hear they're looking for apprentices at Pratt and Gutteridge Panel Beaters. And I'm still young and spry enough to go up the chimneys for the sweeps.'

'Feeling sorry for yourself won't help.'

'Do you think I'm too fat?'

This was a difficult and unfair question to ask Rumana, since she could only answer truthfully. But she was too kind to be undiplomatic.

'Have you thought of becoming a vegetarian?'

They had had this conversation before.

'I'll become a vegetarian when I see a poster of Gandhi over a caption saying, *You too can have a body like mine!'*

Rumana tried to think of someone from Kevin's era who was a vegetarian.

'What about William Shatner?' she said. 'I think he is.'

And so, of course, Kevin mentioned Hitler.

'Anyway,' he added, 'you don't have to be a vegetarian to eat properly.'

'Then eat properly. All you eat is rubbish. Look at all these chocolate wrappers in the bin. You'll end up being ill.' Then she added, 'Perhaps you do need a change of career. What else can you do?'

'I don't know. When I was young, the world really was my oyster. And then I got my foot stuck in a giant clam.'

Rumana didn't ask what the clam was. She knew. Kevin had been dry now for twenty years, and she did not like to bring up the subject of booze.

Kevin looked around the office. The average age was about thirty. Everybody was sitting around chatting. They were all confident and happy. They were all going places. They were only at the beginning of their troubles.

Eventually he had a shaft of inspiration and said, 'If you get a job on a fashion magazine, then you'll be up against other fashion people and you won't be unique. But here you're the *only* textiles and fashion expert.'

'And if I want promotion, I'll have to do something else.'

33

Kevin gave up. He was only just realising how much he loved Rumana and how much he would miss her if she left.

'Are you thinking about getting married?'

'My parents will sort that out.'

'Your par... you mean an arranged marriage? Do they work?'

'Did yours?'

'No. Nothing works. Not even my car. Not even my shaver. That's why I don't have any gym equipment. It wouldn't work. Perhaps I should ask Theo to make me a Peloton. I could provide all the pizza cartons.'

He rubbed his black chin. He had never had a clean shave in his life. There was something to be said for being a castrato, he thought. You didn't get married, you didn't have kids and you never needed to shave. (Although apparently, they did get very fat, so it would be a fool's economy for him.)

'So what would I...I mean what would someone else have to do to marry you?'

'Go and see my parents and make an offer.'

'What's your address?'

'Don't be silly, Kevin. Hadn't you better get on with the Kruddas Prize?'

'I suppose so.' Then he added,

'What are they like, your parents?'

'Kevin, comments are turned off.'

She pointed to his laptop.

'Kruddas Prize.'

Kevin had been putting it off. It was the low spot of his year. He opened his computer and pulled up all the bumf about the literary prize and those writers who had been shortlisted. It was the usual stuff. Year by year he seemed to be reading the same books.

A PASSION FOR GOATS
By
Leonora O'Flanaghan

Set in a rural village in Ireland, it tells the story of retarded shepherdess Mary O' Colveen and the breakdown of her family. Told with passion and intensity, the book courageously faces difficult issues like child abuse and alcoholism. Mary's only solace in life is her pet goat, Maggie. But the family hides a terrible secret. Radio 4 book of the week.

CRY FOR YOURSELF
By Olo Kajinka

Written with passion and intensity and set in the eighties, *Cry for Yourself* tells the story of disabled victim of Apartheid Rana Ngando who emigrates to Thatcher's Britain only to find that her struggles worsen. While there, she starts a family, but her life soon degenerates through alcohol abuse. Radio 4 book of the week.
Highly original and written with passion and intensity – The Guardian

THE BOBBING LOOM
By Lana Turner

Set in the nineteenth century, it deals with the struggles of a mill hand, Bob Roberts, who grows to be an outspoken Trade Union organiser, against the wishes of his family who are afflicted with alcoholism and child neglect. Despite his courage, Roberts' life masks a terrible secret. The novel, written with passion and intensity, makes parallels with Thatcher's Britain in the eighties.

A peerless study of the breakdown of a family – The Harpenden Chronicle.

BELGRANO ROAD

By

Elvira Saffron

Engaging story about a mass murderer who strikes up a friendship with a defrocked nun. A shared interest in the plight of Latin American miners brings them together. But Sister Vera has a terrible secret.

Breath-taking! – Medicine Hat Literary Gazette

OUT!

By Reg Thickpenny

Set in Thatcher's Britain in the eighties, it tells the story of a gay, black Trade Unionist Alan Belgrano. He fights against poverty and inequality while his family struggles against alcohol abuse and child neglect. The novel, written with passion and intensity, ends with his mysterious assassination which the police are reluctant to investigate. Radio 4 book of the week.

Highly original – The Independent

TALK TO THE HAND

By Arnie Gluck

The only American entry to this year's prize, the book's hero is Barney Glucker. Facing loneliness and alienation in New York, Glucker decides to keep a diary of his masturbation fantasies as a response to personal, national and world events. Each week he sends the diary entries to his mother for her comments. Strangely, they grow closer together as a result.

Written with a poetic intensity that I have rarely seen in modern literature. – The New York Times

THIS IS IT!

By Tom Greatorex

Set in Thatcher's Britain in the eighties, the novel tells of Bert Roper, a trade union organiser who takes his family to Alaska to escape Thatcherism. While there, the family is destroyed by alcohol and infighting. Soon, a terrible secret is revealed. Radio 4 book of the week.

At last! A truly original novel! And at 1500 pages, excellent value. -The Independent.

He opened his drawer and pulled out a copy of this week's *Private Eye*, the satirical magazine. They had a send-up of the prize. He looked at theirs and then at the real entries. He could hardly tell the difference. He typed up the satirical entry and placed it on the company intranet mixed up with the real entries. Then he offered a free coffee and doughnut for anyone who could tell which was which. That was a day well spent.

Kevin leaned back in his chair. He had lost the will to live. He had to read all these books. Of course, he wouldn't read them all the way through: that way lay madness. And it would get him blackballed from the Book Reviewers' Club. It was accepted that he would only need to read enough to *give the impression* that he had read them. There was an esoteric art, in which he was well practised, which allowed him to do that. But he must have gone through hundreds of serious modern novels in his life. He had never encountered one that was anywhere near as good as *The Long Goodbye* by Raymond Chandler.

When he had finished, he checked his emails again. there was one from Theo saying,

When you go on your mission, please contact me if you need any help. You know where I am. We are all in this together.

He also included some stuff about a new Soviet wind machine which could blow sand all over western Europe.

Kevin wondered if he could send Theo to Kazakhstan instead. No, that was a wicked thought. He started to pack up. Soon it would be time to go home and talk to his wife. He picked up a copy of *This is it!* to take home and read. The joys of the day multiplied.

He went over to Amis's office to have a word with him about Kazakhstan, but he had gone out. Kevin noticed that Amis was often out in the afternoon.

He checked his phone, which was on mute. His long, sadly-not-lost brother Tom had called and left a message. This was to follow up on the email of the previous week. Tom had another get-rich-quick scheme. Like most people with a taste for get-rich-quick schemes, he suffered from a long, slow burn of indigence, largely caused by a long, slow burn of indolence. Tom's latest wheeze was to sell unwanted personalised number plates to people by giving them the nickname based on the number. So GOZ 1 would be sold to a man known thereafter as Goz. All one needed was the co-operation of his friends, family and work colleagues – but that was a mere detail which could be thrashed out at the first meeting. But first, he needed to find some capital. The idea couldn't fail. Tom's ideas never could, unlike Tom, who perennially did.

Kevin had a sister as well. Her name was Leonora. Kevin resented her for being given the only exotic name in the family. Powered by the glamour it endowed her, she had made a fortune in the marketing profession. Then she had married a lawyer who had even more money, which Kevin thought of as a wasteful and unfair duplication. There was very little likelihood of Leonora calling him, unless it was to sue him.

'Don't go to sleep,' said Kevin's wife, Fiona. She nudged Amis and woke him up.

'What's the matter?' he asked.

'Kevin will be home soon, Geoff. You'd better go.'

Amis got out of bed and started to dress.

'I'm sending him to Kazakhstan for a week. That'll give us more time together,' he said.

'Yes, that will be nice,' she said flatly. She got up herself, put on a robe and started to brush her long, blonde hair.

'Why did you marry a man so much older than yourself?' asked Amis.

'Oh, I did love him,' she said. 'He was very funny. But I just get tired of people.'

'Are you tired of me yet?' he asked. She said nothing.

'It's just that...you seem such an odd couple,' he continued.

'We are. Most people are. The world is full of strange marriages. People marry for lots of reasons. But I bet the most common is that they get fed up with waiting.'

'Probably,' he said. He reached over to kiss her, but she eluded him.

'You really had better go, Geoff.'

'I will.' He started tying his shoes.

'But however ill-matched people are,' she said, 'it's usually something trivial which drives them apart. Paul McCartney used to go out with this model called Jane Asher. I read this in a magazine. She liked to have the window open and he liked to have it closed. Or was it the other way round? He liked to open the window and then she would shut it. Anyway, someone saw this and knew that they wouldn't last. I bet more marriages break up because one of them can't stand doors being open and the other can't stand them shut or something. Or because one of them puts things in the wrong place in the fridge.'

He was ready now. She saw him to the door and they kissed before opening it. Then she opened it a little and checked in the street to make sure no-one was watching. She had seen a very strange looking man hanging about the area recently. He was wearing a false beard. Underneath it was a real beard. She wondered if he was a private detective. Had Kevin paid someone to watch her? This man looked like the sort of detective Kevin would hire.

'I'll call you,' he said. She nodded. Amis left and she closed the door. Yes, she was tired of him. She was tired of a lot of things.

CHAPTER FOUR

On the pretext of preparing to go to central Asia, Kevin left early to visit his mother, who was now 87. She was a resident in the Cheery Twilight Home out in the country. *(A perfect setting in lovely fields and woodland alive with birdsong for those gentle, crepuscular years! Cheery Twilight Homes – for a dignified declination!)*

Madeleine Tregennis was still perfectly compos mentis, although slightly infirm of body. She had all her marbles, but when Kevin arrived the staff couldn't remember which one she was. They had changed her room so many times Kevin wondered if they were expecting an assassination attempt. When he finally found her on the second floor in room 15b, she was sitting up in bed playing a computer game with the young Albanian lad who had brought her the afternoon tea tray. He was sitting in the only chair in the room, so Kevin had to stand while they finished their game.

Budup! Budup! Wssht! Wssht! Budup!

'Hello mother,' he said.

'Oh hello. Now don't tell me…I've seen you before. You're Rumana's friend, aren't you?'

Bzzzt! Wusht!

'Yes, very amusing mother. I'm sorry I haven't been for a while. Did she give you the Turkish Delight?'

Rumana often dropped things off to her when she was passing on the way to her parents' house.

Budup! Wssht! Bleep!

'Was that twenty points, Karl? I'm getting very good at this. Yes, of course she gave me the sweets. Do you think she stole them?'

Wssht! Bleep bleep!

The machine played a ghastly electronic version of *Non Piu Andrai*.

'Is that it, Karl?'

The young lad gracefully admitted that he had been trounced and humiliated. He picked up the tea tray. He nodded coldly at Kevin, as if he had heard terrible things about him, and then left. Kevin sat by the bedside in the seat he had vacated. He could barely get into it.

'Everything all right, mother?'

'Yes, why wouldn't it be? What brings you here?'

She pulled her purple and red bed jacket around her as though she had a chill. In fact, you could have grown mangoes in the room. It was hardly surprising that she was losing weight; the place was like a luxury, labyrinthine Turkish bath. No wonder the chairs were so small.

'Oh, mother don't be like that.'

He plumped up her pillows and she told him to leave them alone.

'I'm not a complete stranger: I do come occasionally. Are they looking after you?'

She placed the gaming consoles on the bedside table and used the zapper to switch off the television. Then she caressed her still beautiful white hair into place. It had been recently styled. There was even a hairdresser on site.

'Of course they're looking after me. They'd better do, the money I pay them. What are you up to?'

'I'm going to Kazakhstan.'

'Kazakhstan? Good grief! Can't you get a job in London?'

'I do have a job in London, mother. What I mean is, the newspaper is sending me to Kazakhstan.'

'Why? What have you done?'

'I haven't done anything...'

But he wasn't actually sure that that was true, so he said,

'That's a good question. I'm not sure. Perhaps I'm too old.'

'Well, I'm eighty-seven and they aren't sending me to Kazakhstan.'

'No, but you don't work for the Globe. Lucky you.'

'How's Fiona?'

'I don't know to be perfectly honest. We don't talk much these days.'

'I told you not to marry her.'

'Yes, but you could still have come to the wedding.'

'I'll come to the next one. You're bound to have more. What number is this? Number two? Whatever happened to Jennifer? I liked her.'

'Yes, I liked her as well, mum, but she ran off with my boss when I was working for the Herald.'

'Oh, yes. I remember him. Trevor – that was his name, wasn't it?'

Her memory was better than his. It always had been.

'I liked him. Handsome devil.'

'Yes, so it would appear.'

'I bet all the women ran after him.'

'Yes, quite possibly,' he said testily.

There was a pause. Then he said,

'So you're all right, then?'

Next time he came, he vowed he would write down some talking points, like a television interviewer.

'Yes, I'm all right, dear.'

Her answer had a distinct undertone of 'no-thanks-to-you'.

Somehow, they got through the allotted visiting time without her dropping off and without too many embarrassing pauses. Then the bell sounded. He got up, kissed her and made to go.

'Oh, by the way,' she said, 'it was your father who liked Turkish Delight. I like sherbet lemons.'

He nodded.

'I'll bring some next time.'

There was no point in saying they were bad for her teeth. She still had every one of hers without so much as one filling. That reminded him: he had to go to the dentist sometime. His mother was 87 and in perfect health while *he* was falling to bits.

He left her and she started up the games console again. He was sure that he felt fond of her. But he couldn't work out if it was the fondness he might feel if she was just any old lady he had volunteered to visit. He had no reference point which would allow him to make a comparison.

When he arrived back home, Fiona said to him:

'Kevin, there's a man here.'

'Good of you to admit it. We shouldn't have any secrets.'

'No, you idiot. He's from the government. The Home Office.'

'The government? Is it about me not voting? I can explain.'

The man who rose from the chair as he entered the sitting room was a very tall, slender, handsome, urbane looking man wearing a suit of breath-taking exquisiteness which had clearly been designed by a team of experts working over several months. He looked like the sort of man Amis wanted to be or thought he was.

The visitor laughed easily.

'Nothing to worry about at all, Mr Tregennis. My name is Danvers. I'm from the Home Office. Is there somewhere we can er... discuss a few things?'

Kevin was mystified.

'There's the box room. It's sort of being converted to a study.'

'It's been converted into a terrible mess,' said Fiona, glaring at Kevin.

'That sounds splendid,' said Danvers. Kevin and Fiona looked at each other in bewilderment.

'I'll make some tea,' she said.

'How very hospitable,' said Danvers. Fiona smiled but looked a little flustered. She was clearly very taken by this sophisticated man in his expensive suit. He had an easy manner and yet was domineering in his personality. Charming and yet with a hint of danger about him. Armed and yet disarming. It had been years since she had seen anyone like him. They didn't have company very often and, lulled into complacency by their unexciting life, she had been caught wearing a track suit. She excused herself and left them.

Kevin led the way upstairs and they both squeezed themselves into the little makeshift study. Kevin sat on the small single bed. Danvers had the rickety office chair.

'Don't tell me,' said Kevin, 'this matter is a little delicate.'

'Most perceptive of you,' said Danvers. 'Firstly, allow me to apologise for my lack of candour with your wife. I'm from the government but not the Home Office. More the bailiwick of the Foreign Office to be exact. Specifically, I'm from MI6.'

Kevin was stunned.

'MI6? You mean you work in that place in Pimlico that looks like the palace of the King of Legoland.'

'Er...yes. Across the river from Pimlico. Now, I'm sure your time is very valuable, Mr Tregennis...'

'Kevin, please...'

'Yes, Kevin,' said Danvers with distaste, as if he had never been trapped in a room with anyone called Kevin before. It was the sort of name his uncle's gamekeeper would be called.

'We understand that you are shortly to be making a trip to Kazakhstan.'

'How the hell did you know that? I only found out about it myself today. Are you bugging my phones?'

'Not at all,' said Danvers with a note of impatience. 'There is a very widely publicised convocation being held there shortly. A lot of papers will be sending people. It was not an inference of Einsteinian proportions to guess that a large and reputable paper like the Globe would be sending someone to cover it. We merely asked the right questions of the right people.'

Danvers shifted uncomfortably on his creaky old chair. One of the casters was loose. It troubled him. He could not look urbane and sophisticated on a chair with a loose caster.

'What's that got to do with the government?'

Danvers tried to get comfortable again. Fiona knocked on the door and came in with a tray of tea and biscuits.

'How lovely,' said Danvers.

'You're lucky.' she said, smiling radiantly at the mysterious guest. 'Kevin normally scoffs all the bourbons as soon as I buy them.'

'Well, how nice of you to bother anyway.'

She put down the tray on the desk and hesitated. Perhaps she was hoping that he would say, 'Please stay, Mrs Tregennis, this concerns you too,' but he didn't. She smiled at him again and left, almost walking backwards as with royalty. By what alchemy she had managed to make tea and change into her best day frock in such a short time, only the forces of darkness knew. She was thirty-seven now but still very attractive. She was a real blonde, which is big medicine for some men. Danvers could watch her go down the stairs from where he was sitting, which he did with the considerable interest of a connoisseur. Then he closed the door and continued.

'A lot of people… businessmen and such like, reporters like yourself, are often courageous and patriotic enough to assist us in one or two of our little endeavours abroad.'

Kevin felt a horrible crawly thing going down his spine, like a mutant choc-ice with hairy legs. It was probably either perspiration or terror. He didn't like that word 'courageous'. It implied all sorts of activities which he had spent his whole life avoiding. Danvers seemed to be aware of his reaction.

'Please don't worry, Kevin. We aren't asking you to get involved in anything dangerous. We have trained personnel for that. Reporters and the like are usually used just for what we call drop-and-collect operations. Letterbox ops. We would simply be asking you to meet one of our operatives in the region and collect something from him.'

Kevin was keen to confirm the most important point.

'You say it won't be dangerous?'

'Not at all, old chum. Just pick it up and bring it home.'

There you go again, thought Kevin. *You're already asking questions as if you've accepted.*

'Pick up what?' he asked.

'Just a very small item. A computer stick.'

'And why can't you do this? Your trained personnel and all.'

'Our professional operatives are well known over there. It would arouse suspicion. Plus, they are very busy. We try to farm out the routine stuff. Now a reporter gathering information... What could be more natural? Incidentally, let me assure you that Kazakhstan is not Iran. It's a reasonably open place.'

'Oh good. And that's all you want me to do? Pick up a computer stick?'

'That's all.'

'And this computer stick contains information which someone else doesn't want us to know.'

'Inevitably the source will have proprietary claims on the data. But that's largely a legal question,' said Danvers with slight irritation as he fidgeted uncomfortably in his chair.

'And who is the source? I mean, looking at the map, it would be difficult not to assume that it could be Russia.'

He had done it again.

'Well, I'm impressed. I had no idea that you knew so much about the area. You know, I really must congratulate you, Kevin. You are one jump ahead of me. But really the risk is minimal. Just pick up the stick and take it to your hotel. One of us will then arrange to collect it. It won't be in your possession for more than an hour. Any questions?'

'Yes, if this computer stick contains information that can be put on a computer, why not just email it to you?'

'Good grief man! You must be joking. Splash it all over the internet like Poundsaver bodywash? That would be a disaster. There would be no limit to who could access it. The papers might get hold of it.'

'But I work for the papers.'

'Yes, but you will also be signing the Official Secrets Act before I leave, won't you?'

'Will I? Yes, I suppose so.'

Kevin thought for a while. They both had some tea and a biscuit. Danvers had invoked patriotism and courage. Kevin had more of the former than the latter. He didn't like spies and spying. He thought it was a grubby and nasty little world. But he supposed that someone had to do it. And it might be important to the country, which, tired old cynic that he pretended to be, was an important consideration for him. There was a picture of the late Queen on the wall. She seemed to be smiling at him as though she had great faith in him.

'All right. I'll pick up your computer stick for you.'

'Excellent. Good. First class chap,' said Danvers, taking out a piece of paper like some insurance salesman. Kevin signed it with a biro that didn't work. He fumbled around in the drawer for another and signed it properly. Danvers, who had to countersign the document, provided his own. Kevin was prepared to bet that he always had or did or said the right thing at the right time. Then, the spymaster got up to go, smiling his smile of easy conquest.

'Excellent. Now...any questions before I leave?'

'I don't think so. Aren't you going to give me an exploding code book or an inflatable radio transmitter hidden in a red surgical sock?'

'No. No, we weren't planning to. Can you envisage any situation where you might need such items?'

'I hope not.'

'Intelligence work is about gathering information, Kevin. It's not at all like those silly films and books. It's just about keeping up with what the other side is doing.'

'Other side? Is there another side nowadays?'

'Well, the others then.'

'What if the others have invented an exploding code book?'

'Yes, well, I've taken up a great deal of your time. You'll be contacted about your meeting place within the next two days. You won't hear from me again.'

Well, that's something, thought Kevin, but he just smiled.

They shook hands and went downstairs. Danvers thanked Fiona for her hospitality with what Kevin thought was unnecessary fulsomeness. Fiona, who had by now put on her full make-up, was beaming like a schoolgirl meeting the King. He was most welcome. He must come again. She managed to stop herself saying, 'When Kevin isn't here.' And then he left.

Fiona stopped smiling.

'I have never been so embarrassed in my life,' she shouted.

'Why? What's wrong? I didn't know he was coming.'

'Taking him upstairs to that dump! Why don't you clear that study up? And put a caster on that chair. Do you realise he could sue us if he fell off?'

'What else could I do? Take him to the Rose and Crown?'

And so on, until she reminded him to do the front lawn. Kevin was glad to oblige. He went round the back of their semi and opened the side gate. Then he hauled the rattletrap little push-mower onto the grass at the front. He was happy to do the lawn. He loved repetitive work that he could lose himself in without thinking about his problems or himself. Or even Rumana.

There was a great book by Albert Camus called *La Peste* or *The Plague*. Kevin had studied it for 'A' level French. In it, an old bedridden man passed the time by counting out dried peas from one pan to another. Then, when he had finished, he counted them back into the first pan, day in, day out. There had been much discussion in class about what this signified. But Kevin had understood. He could empathise with any mind-numbing activity which muffled the ticking of the sneering clock of life until it was all mercifully over. Counting peas or mowing the lawn was as good a method as any. Reading French literature was another, of course.

He pushed the crummy old mower back and forth in an exact straight line, knowing that in a few weeks he would have to do it again. That prospect soothed him. There would always be a fresh supply of grass to be mowed, back and forth, to no purpose, until the end of time. Or at least until winter. In the garden, his life flowed gently, hypnotically and purposelessly past, pea by miserable pea.

After cutting half of the lawn, he went inside to get a soft drink. Fiona was sitting on the sofa leafing through some sort of home-and-garden-type magazine. She had opened a bottle of red wine and filled up a glass big enough to have trodden the grapes in. Her bushy blonde hair was tied up in some kind of wide psychedelic headscarf, like one of the acts at Woodstock. She had changed into a pair of stretch pants which were the same colour. She didn't acknowledge him, but took a huge gulp of the blood red juice. Fiona liked wine. Kevin didn't. He had never forgiven red wine for not tasting like Ribena. He struggled to think of something that he and Fiona had in common. They had liked each other once. How strange to discover that this was not enough. You had to have something in common. Difficult as it was to believe, the world of eternal romance and devotion belonged to the stamp collectors, the caravaners, the brass rubbers and the ballroom dancers.

He could tell she was in a baleful mood. She was listening to her one-hit wonder song, recorded when she was only 18. It was a novelty number called *Give Me Your Doo-Dabs, Mistah.* She had performed under the exotic sobriquet of Missy-Bee. The song had enjoyed a modicum of success in the dance clubs of the time and reached number six in some obscure subset chart. Her second offering had been a pretty song called *See Through Love.* It had combined a thoughtful lyric with a string arrangement which had attracted critical attention. It had bombed like a flight of old Lancasters.

For five years after she had chased the ever-fading dream, appearing in ever more obscure clubs, first as a singer and then as a backing singer for other singers who were two or three years behind her on the slippery downward snake. In 2010, she gave up show business completely. It was the same year that she had met Kevin. She had recently taken to calling it The Year My Life Ended when talking to friends.

Kevin looked at her and was about to say something, but he decided he didn't have anything to say. He went back outside and was just in time to see the scrap metal collectors' van disappearing around the corner with his lawn mower in the back.

Kevin ran to his car – a second hand Alfresco. It was parked on the grass verges outside his house. He removed a neighbour's note from the windscreen which read, 'You have left tyre tracks on the grass – again!' and jumped in. He tried to do a three-point turn with some bonus points added and sped off in pursuit of the lorry. But there was no sign of it. He drove around and around in circles until he got a powerful feeling of déjà vu. When he got back, the neighbour who had left the note had parked in the exact same spot.

When he got back inside, Fiona was asleep in the chair and snoring like a bison. She had been watching a quiz programme on television.

No, Madge, that's not correct. The Brothers Karamazov were not acrobats. I'm afraid you lose your £200 bonus payment. But you don't go away empty handed. Here's your Wheel of Destiny sock bag…

Kevin sat on the edge of the sofa and looked tenderly at his wife for a while. He was sure that he had loved her once and that she had loved him. He thought of their wedding. She had seemed so happy. Surely, she couldn't have been faking it? No, some people do, but she was not insincere, just mercurial. And she was no gold digger. If she was, she wouldn't have married into a derelict, open-cast tin mine like him.

No, Sandra, the answer is not Elvis Presley. You're thinking of Heartbreak Hotel. Heartbreak House was written by George Bernard Shaw…Easy mistake to make, though…

Where had their love gone, he thought? There was no more enduring and agonising mystery in the universe. Perhaps deep emotions couldn't survive in life. Perhaps they just got smothered in the encroaching sea of oppressive daily trivia.

No, I'm sorry, The Idiot *was not written by Jilly Cooper, but a good guess though…so Jim Thomas, sociology lecturer…your only chance now to survive is to risk everything by spinning the… Wheel of Destiny…!*

'Don't do it, Jim,' said Kevin. 'Take the money and go home. Always take the money.'

Kevin slept fitfully that night. Thoughts of Kazakhstan, spying, redundancy and danger spiced with Rumana swirled around in his head. He used up a lot of energy in his life fearing for the worst. The worst always came, and when it did, he had no energy left to face it.

Kevin asked Rumana if she wanted to go to the zoo before he left for the mighty, rolling plains of central Asia. He was amazed when she said yes, but less shocked when she added,

'As long as you don't read anything into it.'

He promised that he wouldn't, although he knew he lied. He was excited by the opportunity to talk to Rumana alone. She was a very friendly person but was of a very quiet and shy disposition. She never really initiated a conversation with other people, except to complain about the latte machine not working. And while this was a regular occurrence, it was not enough to form the basis of a flourishing relationship.

They went to Regent's Park Zoo. On the way in they were barracked by animal rights protesters. A sign of the times. So much violence dressed up as tolerance and concern. They seemed to hate humans more than they loved animals. But there were enough naive people in the world to take them at face value.

Once inside, they ambled about with no particular plan, looking here and there at the inmates. The chimpanzees were the most interesting study. They both stared at the chimps and the chimps stared back. It may have been a delusion, but Kevin thought he could sense a kind of dignified awareness on their part. It was as if they were thinking, *We may live in trees and eat our own excrement, but at least we're not being sent to Kazakhstan shortly.* They were right, of course, he thought. They had ordered their lives well. They were staying in London and he was going to the back of beyond, which is where the chimps had started life. It was clear that they were going up while Kevin was losing his way. He and Rumana watched for a while and then walked on. They didn't speak for a few moments until suddenly she said,

'What animal would you be, then?'

'Do I have to be an animal?'

56

'Oh, yes. You must. What would you be?'

'Oh, that's easy: an alligator.'

'A what? An alligator? Oh, my goodness!'

'When I went to Florida, the high spot of the trip was seeing *Gatorland* in Orlando. I preferred it to *Seaworld*, although I have nothing against dolphins.'

'How horrid. Eurghh. I hate alligators. What a surprising answer. I never expected you to say that.'

'And what did you expect me to say? A chimpanzee, I suppose.'

'No...no, of course not,' she said guiltily. 'Why alligators?'

'Well, they don't mess about, you know. If they don't like you, they tell you. There's something to be said for that. There's a brutal honesty about reptiles that you have to admire. Don't you like me a little?'

'Kevin, you promised.'

'I said 'like'. I only said 'like'. Anyway, I had cross kings when I promised.'

'I like you a lot. Just not in that way.'

'The way you like chimps or *Strictly Come Dancing*. Why don't you love me?'

'Oh, Kevin, honestly. You're too old.'

'You mean too fat and too bald?'

'And too old as well.'

They walked on in more silence, he, hoping against hope, that she would hold his arm. She didn't. They stopped and bought ice creams at a kiosk. Eventually he said,

'Go on. What animal would you be?'

'Guess.'

'I don't know. A panda.'

'A panda? Interesting. Yes, I might want to be a panda.'

She smiled at him. It was like the sun coming out on the first day of spring.

'Why? Because they're cuddly or because they're rare? Do you see yourself as an endangered species?'

'Everything's an endangered species, including us. Anyway, I like pandas because they're nice and quiet. And they don't bother anyone.'

'That's all you know. Pandas support Millwall. The police arrest more pandas for football violence than any other animal.'

'Really? I've never seen that in the papers.'

'Of course you haven't. They suppress it. They can't upset significant interest groups.'

'I didn't think pandas were such a powerful lobby.'

'No, but the Chinese are. They don't want to lose a lot of valuable trading contracts.'

'And what about alligators? Who do they support?'

'This is what I'm saying to you: they're misunderstood. Most of them prefer handicrafts and chess. Or Chinese pottery.'

She laughed. He laughed. The sun really came out. It was a beautiful and delightful day for Kevin. It was a frustrating and agonising one for him. Rumana just thought it was a nice day out with a friend. She knew nothing of his turmoil. Here he was with her, the object of his desires, for a whole morning - and yet he might just as well be at the North Pole for all the good it was doing. So close and yet bloody miles away. Just like Kazakhstan. Just like everything. The chimps were winning.

They left the zoo after about an hour and walked back to Rumana's car. On the drive back, he asked her if she wanted to go to the cinema some time.

'Kevin, please! You're married!'

'That's OK: she'll let me have some money. If not, I'll steal it out of her purse while she's at her cage fighting class.'

'No! And don't ask me again. Anyway, you'll be in Asia.'

'Well, they have cinemas in Kazakhstan. If you want to pop over we can go and see *The Triumph of Irrigation over the Desert*. They remade it with Julie Andrews but the original is better. There's a cameo of Stalin in it.'

'Always the way with the classics.'

And so the day ended. It had been sunny, warm, gentle and inviting. And Rumana had been with him. All the ingredients for perfection were present and yet the perfection had eluded him, like an immaculate chain of reasoning leading to an absurd and contradictory conclusion. The day had been a painstakingly prepared but collapsed souffle.

Two days later, Rumana drove him to the airport. Fiona only worked part-time as a librarian in the nearby town, but she had been unaccountably busy. So was Amis, who had not been there when Kevin had left. Not that Kevin cared.

'So, how's the job-hunting going?'

'Great. I've got a job.'

'What?' said Kevin, suddenly affected by psychosomatic laryngitis. 'A what?'

'I'll be handing in my resignation tomorrow.'

'Oh, I see. Was it written with passion and intensity?'

'It certainly was. It's going to be Radio 4's resignation of the week.'

'Oh dear. When will you leave?'

'Two weeks. I can't wait.'

'Two weeks,' he intoned, as if at a funeral. 'It will drag for you but fly by for me. That's relativity according to Einstein.'

'Yes, I'm going to *Art and Stuff*. I'll be the new fashion editor.'

Kevin was crushed. He was a fifty-year-old hack and she was an editor at less than thirty.

'The Globe offered me more money, but I said no.'

'Good for you. You can't be bought.'

'Yes, I can, but it wasn't enough. They wouldn't give me what I asked.'

'So young and so ruthless. You should be a spy. Would you like to go to Kazakhstan?'

'Not really. Couldn't *you* ask them for more money?'

'There's no need: I have a paper round on the side. I both write the news and deliver it. That's called vertical integration. I give lectures on the subject. George Soros saw one and said we should have lunch some time.'

Rumana had no idea what he was talking about, but Kevin chuntered on. He was a man in conflict. His main preoccupation of the moment was *Can I kiss her goodbye at the airport?*

As though she were reading his mind she said,

60

'Oh by the way, I'm engaged as well.'

'Engaged? You're engaged?' he said, sounding like a small boy in a deep, dark well.

She showed him the ring. He adored her and he hadn't noticed it.

'Yes. Aren't you going to congratulate me?'

'No. No, I don't think I could bring myself to do that. I really wouldn't mean it. When did this terrible and ill-advised event occur?'

'My parents told me last night.'

'What a nice surprise for you. This is turning out to be a great week. If only my luggage would go missing. Only then will my happiness be complete.'

He leaned back in the seat of the pool car.

'I feel shattered.'

'You can sleep on the plane.'

'Not really. I have to change at Ankara. Anyway, there's bound to be chaos with the flights at the moment. The French air traffic controllers aren't on strike and it's causing confusion with the airlines. They build their schedules around the assumption that they will be.'

'How long are you away?' she said, just to shut him up.

'Just a few days. Could you look in on my mother while I'm away? See if she wants anything.'

'Of course.'

There was an awkward pause, so she said,

'What about your father? You never talk about him.'

'I never really knew him. He walked out on us when I was seven. And he wasn't there much before that. Apparently, he liked Turkish Delight. That's the only piece of solid information I have about him.'

'That's terrible. I mean about walking out, not about the Turkish Delight. Where is he now?'

'No idea. I'm sure he'll turn up when I'm rich and famous. They usually do. Full of remorse and 'You were too young to explain myself at the time' and can I lend him two hundred quid? He's probably scouring the pages of *Hello Magazine* and the celebrity sections of the tabloids looking for clues to my whereabouts as we speak.'

'That's very sad.'

'Yes, it's very sad.'

'Anyway,' she said, 'I hear Kazakhstan is lovely. There's a lot of oil wealth there and they've built lots of new hotels and stuff in the capital.'

'I had no idea you knew so much about it. Are you sure you wouldn't like to go?'

She said nothing to this, so he said,

'Oil wealth is irrelevant. It doesn't make a country rich. There are plenty of countries with gas and oil who aren't rich. There's probably a fifty-foot gold statue of the president in the middle of the square. The rest of the money all ends up in a numbered Swiss chocolate factory. Or in a Docklands office block shaped like a human foot.'

He rattled away in this fashion until they arrived at Heathrow. She dropped him off in the car park. He leaned over and fumbled the kiss as he had known he would. She turned away at the last moment and he kissed her hair. He would have to make do with that.

'By the way, Kevin,' she said as he was getting out, 'which ones were the real book reviews?'

'All of them,' he said.

After a processing routine that would have been appropriate to joining the Wagner Group, Kevin made it to the British Airways plane and to his seat. There had been no copies of the *Globe* available at the WH Smith concession, so he had bought a copy of the Guardian to read during the flight. Once in the air, he gazed idly at the articles.

Children Should Swear at their Parents, says Expert.
Report - Brexit Menopause Stress Higher in Lesbians
What Fish Can Teach Us About Racism
My Child's Kindergarten Won't Discuss Genocide
Why won't the Media Talk about Scabies?
The Forgotten Women of Azerbaijani Cinema

Gradually his eyes closed and he fell into a long but troubled sleep.

When he awoke, his copy of the Guardian had disappeared from his lap. A ferocious-looking man sitting across the aisle was reading it with disturbed intensity. Kevin said nothing. He was a great one for leaving Destiny to punish such people. Perhaps this was a coward's philosophy. Well, why shouldn't they have one? Cowards make good philosophers. Of necessity, they are prepared to spend the requisite amount of time and energy on those vital fatalistic speculations.

British Airways got Kevin to Turkey with a minimum of fuss, apart from the usual delays on the ground. There was another hold-up at Ankara which was long enough to make Kevin wonder whether they were actually building the connecting plane from scratch. This was not to be wondered at, since the airline which took him from Ankara to Kazakhstan was Aeroflot. Once Aeroflot had been the national airline of Kazakhstan, back in the days of Soviet satrapy. Now the country was free from Russian bondage, but the Aeroflot planes still went to any country which did not ask too many awkward questions about airworthiness and safety.

Aeroflot planes are not always lethal, but they certainly are character building. Once in the air, the plane was as cold as a Birdseye Storage Depot. The stewardess – whose name was Katya and would have been a model, had she been born in the West - explained that this was only caused by a small problem with the thermostat. This was a great relief to Kevin, who had wondered at one time whether there were holes in the fuselage. The plane got into the air and managed to travel in the right direction. This seemed to be enough for most of the passengers and Kevin was glad that the spirit of intrepidity was still alive in other countries.

He was sitting next to a man big enough to dam a river. The man had introduced himself as Orli or something. Kevin had no idea which country he was from, but he was reading a book of chess puzzles in English. After half an hour Orli said,

'Do you play chess?'

'No. Not anymore. The doctor says I have to take it easy at my age.'

Orli stared at him.

'It's getting the pieces out of the box that's the dangerous bit.'

Orli took a few seconds to process this piece of information and then went back to his puzzles. Katya came and gave them an inflight meal which would have started a riot in the Roman army. Kevin had no idea what was in it, but suspected potatoes had formed the conceptual basis. The giant chess man ate his in almost one mouthful and returned to his book. Kevin gathered that he didn't fly a lot. He hadn't got that big on aeroplane food.

There was a little screen in the back of the seat in front plus a pair of headphones. Kevin donned the headset and looked at the selection of films. They were all in Russian. He chose the one whose write-up had the most exclamation marks. It wasn't easy to tell whether he was watching a drama, a comedy or a soap opera, but he thoroughly enjoyed the bad acting. There is something greatly universal about bad acting which transcends all social and linguistic barriers. No wonder the French, those eternal internationalists, put such great store by it.

CHAPTER FIVE

Kazakhstan is just underneath Russia, so by comparison it doesn't look that big. It is actually enormous. It is four and a half times as big as the Ukraine which means basically too many football pitches to be a meaningful measure. It is also one of the most sparsely populated countries in the world. This means that it would be a great place to sit out World War Three. There is nothing to bomb and a million square miles of that nothing. There is oil wealth, but there is not much else for the population to do except to weave traditional tapestry and wait to be invited to take part in the Eurovision Song Contest.

Kevin could see the airport of Astana, formerly Nur-Sultan, from the window of the plane. He had to peep across the man sitting in the window seat, no mean feat given his ability to blot out the sun. Kevin was normally terrified of looking out of plane windows but as they were coming in to land, it was not so bad.

There was no sign anywhere of a fifty-foot golden statue of the president, although he could see a bizarre structure which appeared to represent a hand holding a golden ball. Worth every penny they paid for that, he thought. Perhaps there had been a statue but it had been toppled. Statues have a tendency to get thrown down in the modern world. Far-sighted leaders would make them out of rubber. Except there was probably more gold in the country than rubber. He scoured the city for other points of interest. But soon all he could see was the airport and that looked like every other airport in the world.

As they left the plane, Katya gave him a lovely smile. Kevin liked her but felt sorry for her, as he felt sorry for anyone on the frontline of customer service in a moribund industry. She probably spent her entire life apologising. In another life she would have been fighting off millionaires with a blackjack, instead of being a harassed functionary on the Airline That Time Forgot. He had feared the worst about luggage, but today was his lucky day, and there it was waiting for him on the carousel. This was too good for comfort. He went in search of transport. The hotel in Astana was called the Hotel Astana, so there was no doubt that Kevin had landed in the right place. The taxi driver of Astana Taxis had confirmed it.

The place was impressive and luxurious enough. He was ashamed to admit that he had expected something far worse. No doubt motivated by the basest kinds of prejudice, he had anticipated that a five star hotel in this part of the world meant that the lice powder was brought up on a silver platter. After all, the country had once been a Soviet colony and he had heard all the horror stories about hotels under the former communist regime, where anything less than three stars was part of the Gulag system. But not a bit of it. The reception was spacious enough to hold a netball match and while the marble fittings were probably more acrylic and cement than the genuine article, it looked very salubrious and welcoming. There were three lifts and all of them appeared to be working. This was a miracle that even the hotels of the West failed to pull off.

To the right of the plush lobby was a lounge bar. (Kazakhstan, although mainly Muslim, had once had the mores of her northern neighbour imposed on her, so whatever else was forbidden or in short supply, there was no prohibition of alcohol.)

Inside the bar, whooping it up like cowboys, were the American oilmen of Chevron. Most of the exploration and the oilfields were over to the West around the shore of the Caspian Sea, so these guys were obviously on furlough and were making the most of it. They were making sure that their work colleagues back West could hear them having fun. (Actually, they weren't having fun: they were just drunk. They *thought* they were having fun. That's one of the effects of alcohol.) As he passed by, one of them caught sight of him and shouted, 'Hey Englishman. Come on and have a beer!'

'How did you know I was English?' asked Kevin, which caused much riotous amusement. It was as though a man in a ten-gallon hat with spurs and buffalo dung on his boots had said, 'How did you know I was American?'

They were a mixed bunch these oilmen, but they were all Good Ole Boys from the Deep South. Whatever else may be said about Americans, nobody faults them on their generosity and hospitality. They again invited Kevin to have a beer with them.

'We know how much you guys drink over there in the UK,' said one of them.

'I used to,' explained Kevin, 'but not anymore. What I need at the moment is some rest.'

He thanked them and then went to reception to get his key and then went upstairs. He hoped his room was a long way away from the bar. He put the plastic key card in his pocket and realised that there was a piece of paper in it. He took it out. It was a set of instructions for the meeting. Who had put it there? Orli, no doubt. Or maybe Katya? He liked to think it had been Katya. That would have been more in line with what he expected from espionage work. A beautiful but demonic spy with a big diamond ring full of knock-out drops. She would give him the password, *I must sleep with you immediately*, to which his coded response would be, *I am sorry; I must take my galoshes to the repair shop*.

Once unpacked in his suite, he opened his laptop. He wanted to send an email to Rumana and to his wife. Nothing excessive for Rumana, just light and chatty. Don't overdo it, he thought. Then he undressed and went to bed. He slept until his phone told him it was time to get up. After he had showered and dressed, he went down to the hotel foyer, only to find that a free taxi was waiting for him.

The Astana Conference Hall was in the middle of a new development in the centre of the city. Some of the older buildings displayed the dead hand of the Soviet early, middle and late Concrete Period. Others, newer, showed what happened when Japanese architects are given too much money, drugs and complete artistic freedom: buildings which looked like hypertrophied executive toys. Two eras jostled for space and recognition. Neither appeared to be winning.

He had no trouble finding the venue. The amphitheatre looked like a giant round vegetable steamer from the outside. This was probably the first time it had ever been filled. Kevin guessed that it was one of those vanity projects, built on cheap loans, designed to pump up the GDP figures. Just like the roads to nowhere in Saudi Arabia and the empty towns in China. The arena was far too large for most conferences, unless the Pope wanted to use it to address every single Catholic in

Eurasia. Kevin couldn't see the Pope coming to Kazakhstan. Not unless it was for a penance.

He entered the conference hall and obtained a free cup of coffee which, by an oversight, was not called Astana coffee. As he settled himself in the luxurious velvet seating – clearly the designers had understood that the main requirement of the average conference attendee was a good day's sleep - he was given a glossy brochure for free entitled *New Horizons for Humanity* or *The New Enlightenment*. No expense had been spared – which is often the way when nobody is accountable for the expenditure. The hall soon filled up and some people seemed very friendly. Kevin wondered if perhaps it wouldn't be so bad.

After an introduction from some UN functionary whose name Kevin couldn't hear or pronounce, the first speaker came on. She was an 'expert in inclusive language' from Indonesia. Kevin had never heard of any such occupation. She spoke in a brain curdling monotone for a mere one and a half hours. The gist of her paper was that the pronoun 'he' was colonial and oppressive and therefore genocidal. Instead of pelting her with rotten fruit as Kevin had expected, the audience gave her a standing ovation.

After she had finished, there was a break during which the audience filed out of the hall and into the atrium where they were treated to a buffet, the sumptuousness of which would have shamed the former Shah of Persia. After people had eaten more than their bodies could hold and could eat no more, they filed back in and listened to the second speaker. This was an American woman who gave her name as Inner

70

City 3. She had a more upbeat message entitled *Real Freedom Now – Start with your Kids.*

"My partner Earthgirl and I teach our children, 'You are the most important person in the world. Nobody is more important than you are. Nobody can tell you what to do. You are a free agent without responsibility to anyone but yourself. Do what you want all the time and be accountable to no-one else. Don't even listen to me if you don't want to.'"

She only spoke for three quarters of an hour, which was a great relief to Kevin but not to anyone else. Once again, instead of being tarred and feathered for her blasphemy, she was applauded to the point of exhaustion for her wisdom. How could anyone think that this was a recipe for anything other than turning children into demons? Was he the only sane person in the room? Then there was another break for more culinary excess.

During this second interval, as they all tucked into yet another feast of Caligulan proportions, he got chatting with a very approachable Latin American woman called Elia. She was dressed in what appeared to be two burgundy velvet curtains from an old British cinema screen. Her hat was made from the same material but a different colour. They introduced themselves.

'And may I ask what you do?'

'I'm from the Globe. A British newspaper.'

That made her take a step back. It was a bit like going to a Hollywood orgy and meeting someone who said he was a professional

71

blackmailer. Kevin could see her wondering if she had said anything compromising so far. But she was a diplomat, so she said,

'How fascinating. It must be wonderful to live by words.'

'Yes, I'm struggling with a novel at the moment.'

'Oh, how very interesting. Have you written much?'

'I'm not writing it, I'm reading it. It's one of the Kruddas Prize entries.'

'Aaah, what I would not give to have such literary talent.'

She was too nice and polite for him to say, 'You're bloody kidding me, aren't you?', so he just smiled and agreed with her.

'Are you finding the speeches quite fascinating?'

'Well, I think intriguing is the word I would use. I'm a student of psychology.'

She couldn't agree more but she had just seen someone she knew and had to go. But it was lovely to have met him. Then it was announced that the last speaker was taking the podium, so back in they went.

The last speaker turned out to be a Taiwanese software engineer from Los Angeles who gave a mercifully short talk of half an hour, on how computer software could assist people to 'progress themselves'. This programme added up to people allowing their thoughts to be monitored by Artificial Intelligence for political heresy. Again, he was almost buried in palms and drowned out with hosannahs.

'Isn't this illuminating?' said a man next to Kevin. He could only agree that he had gained an important insight into human nature. He was drained with despair and could barely speak or walk as he made his way out of the hall.

Outside, there was a big crowd of people milling about. A taxi pulled up but they ignored it. They were probably expecting stretch limos with swimming pools in the back filled with champagne and asses' milk. Elton John would have felt right at home here, although he probably would have felt guilty as well.

Arriving back at the hotel, he had only just walked into the reception when the good ole boys – were they still there from yesterday? - spotted him and shouted,

'Hey Englishman! You changed your mind about that beer?'

Kevin, his senses numbed to the point of stupefaction by what he had just experienced, made the worst mistake of his life.

'Yes,' he replied, 'I bloody have.'

They all cheered and whooped and welcomed him into their nascent Bacchanalia. He started with a beer. Then he had another one.

Alcohol has a certain effect on some people and they should never drink. Kevin only had to have one sip and he was a different person, as though he had been drinking all day.

He had another beer. They all Yee-haaahed. They introduced themselves. Someone was called Jimbo and someone was called Billy. Perhaps two of them were called Billy. Unless one of them was called Billy-Joe Jimbo. Then they had some whiskey. Then Kevin started asking in a loud voice while banging the bar, what kind of American saloon this was if they didn't slide the redeye down the counter, eh? They whooped and happily obliged. Kevin dropped some of them but drank the ones he caught. They all laughed and went yee-haaah. Then they suggested some karaoke. Kevin was all up for that. He began to sing his speciality karaoke song *My Way*. *My Way* wasn't the piece of music that they were playing on the karaoke machine, but he didn't care anymore. A convert to the philosophy of Albert Camus after the torments of the day, he decided that life was now absurd.

Oddly enough, the next song they played *was My Way,* so Kevin started singing *Knees up Mother Brown*. The Americans had never heard such a song before and were most appreciative. He showed them how to dance a knees-up and they all did. Kevin tried to buy a round but they wouldn't hear of it. The drink flowed. Kevin could not remember at what point he decided to do a strip on the table. All he knew was that by the time he got to his hotel room, he was reduced to a shameless, prelapsarian nakedness. He didn't care.

Giggling stupidly, he had a brainwave. He picked up his phone – which one of the men who had carried him back had been kind enough to put by his bedside along with his wallet and clothes.

'Hello,' said a quiet voice.

'Rumana?'

'Yes. Who is this? Is that Kevin? Are you all right?'

'I'm as right as a little spring bunny rabbit, my dearest darling. How are you this fine evening?'

'I'm still at work. Kevin, you're not drunk. are you?'

'I must admit I've had a tiny little tincture of the creature, and I'm all the better for it let me tell you.'

He sniggered.

'Oh, Kevin, you don't sound it. What time is it over there? I should think it's late, isn't it? You need to get to bed, Kevin.'

'I need to get to bed all right.'

He cackled like a moustachioed villain in a melodrama.

'I need to be all tucked up with you, my little French truffle.'

'Oh, Kevin stop it! Anyway, I'm not French, I'm Pakistani. Have a shower and go to sleep.'

Kevin had a mood swing.

'Oh, Rumana – I love you. Why don't you love me?'

'I can't, Kevin. I'm engaged. And you're twice my age.'

'I never used to be. I was young once. I can be young again, Rumana.'

But she put the phone down. He wept and sobbed on the bed. Then he guiltily put on his dressing gown as if he had somehow exposed himself to her.

He tried calling her again, but she didn't answer. Then he began to think. Tomorrow night he had to go and meet his contact. He didn't want to. He was afraid. Afraid and lonely and fed up. And then he had a dubious drunken brainwave. He rummaged in his jacket pocket and found Theo's card. Then he dialled.

'Yes?' said a suspicious voice.

'Theo?'

'Who's that?'

'I can't say. You know who I am.'

'Of course, of course. It's Kevin Tregennis, isn't it?'

That's my Theo, thought Kevin.

'Listen to me, Theo. I'm on that mission I told you about. Things have gone a bit awry.'

'Ah yes,' said Theo. 'I understand.'

Kevin could hear him nodding.

'Good. I need you to come here. I'm in Kazakhstan.'

'Is that on the bus route?'

'No, it's a country, Theo. A country in the former…in the Soviet bloc. I need you to take a plane here.'

'Now? It's my bath night.'

'There are some things, Theo, which are more important than bath night. And espionage is one of them,' he said portentously. 'You have a passport, don't you?'

Of course he had a passport. In case the balloon went up.

He gave Theo his instructions, making sure that he wrote them down. It took Theo some time to find his notebook.

'Put the notebook in your pocket now and don't lose it.'

'I'm not a beginner, you know.'

'Theo,' said Kevin, trying to sound like Harrison Ford, 'I wouldn't be asking you if you were.'

'And shall I bring the you-know-what machine?'

Kevin had no idea what he was talking about.

'Yes, but be careful going through customs.'

Theo hung up. He had a serene smile on his face. The call had finally come.

CHAPTER SIX

Kevin slept late the next day. He had missed the second day of the conference, but he hadn't intended to go anyway. It took him a good twenty minutes from regaining consciousness to get to where he could sit up in bed. Then he lay down again. After a while he managed to gather the strength to look at his watch. There was a knock at the door. He ignored it. Then there was another knock and a voice said, 'Cleaner'. 'Go away. Not now,' he said. He crawled off to the toilet. Then he went back to bed and fell asleep.

He was awoken much later by another knock. This knock had a special personality all of its own. It went knock-knock, knockety-knock, knock knock knock. Then when Kevin didn't answer, it kept repeating like a death-watch beetle's distress signal. Eventually, Kevin got up, pulled on his bathrobe, staggered across the room and opened the door.

Theo was standing there.

'Theo!!? What on earth are you doing here?'

'But you called me. You told me to come. The mission.' Then he said, 'Aaah, yes I see!'

He had realised that Kevin was feigning ignorance of Theo's part in the affair in case anyone was listening.

'You'd better come in,' said Kevin.

Theo came into the room and put down his hastily packed bags. He must have brought everything in his house bar the washing machine. Kevin, exhausted by this massive expenditure of effort, plumped down on the bed. He felt like a bomb had exploded in his head.

'Sit down, Theo. Now, a little note about spy craft. Two points, hardly worth mentioning – but they could save your life.'

Theo nodded enthusiastically.

'First, there is not much use in having a secret knock if the people on the other side of the door haven't been told what it is. And secondly, there is no need to wear a false beard if you already have a real beard. If a man with a beard wants to disguise himself, he is usually better advised to shave it off.'

Theo fumbled inside his coat pockets. He seemed to be searching for a notebook.

'Don't bother to write it down, I'm preparing some notes for you. Then we'll have questions later on.'

'Ah, thank you,' said Theo. He sat down in the chair by the window. He had a very keen but nervous look.

'What is it you want me to do?' asked Theo.

'Let me get myself organised first and then we'll have a chat. My head is screaming at me.

'You weren't drunk, were you?' asked Theo, scandalised at the thought. 'You are on duty, you know.'

'It's my job to make contacts and socialise with people…but Theo…'

He looked to each side before continuing.

'…I think I may have been drugged.'

Theo's eyes opened wide. He understood everything.

Kevin invited Theo to make a cup of coffee for them both while he went into the bathroom for some full-scale ablutions. When he came back, Theo had made the coffee and left the countertop in a complete mess.

More of the coffee and milk was on the outside of the cups than inside. He had chosen his accomplice well.

They both sat down again and Kevin went over what his mission was and what he wanted Theo to do. Of course, he had been drunk when he called Theo but that couldn't be helped now. And anyway, Danvers had made it very clear that this was not a dangerous assignment. Just a piece of meet-and-collect or drop-and-pickup or whatever the phrase had been. A computer key, that was all.

Theo assured Kevin that he could be trusted to do it. He asked Kevin to repeat all the details several times, just to be sure that he had them correctly. Or, as Kevin suspected, because he had forgotten them or not understood them. After that, he took Theo down to have breakfast, which actually turned out to be dinner. Theo was very suspicious that the waiters were speaking Russian.

'It's for that reason that we must be careful,' Kevin told him.

Back in the room, Theo insisted on showing Kevin his spy detector.

'I think you've already shown it to me.'

'Oh, no, you must let me demonstrate it.'

Kevin went over to the kettle to make some more coffee – he didn't even trust Theo to do that. While his back was turned, the other man fumbled with one of his bags and pulled out the incredible contrivance. As he did so, the bicycle lamp attachment caught on the faulty zip of the bag. The light came on. It was pointing straight at Kevin. Theo was horrified.

Oh no!! he thought, *Tregennis is a spy!*

Kevin turned and smiled at him. Theo smiled back. He would need all his tradecraft and cunning for this unexpected scenario.

*****

It was getting cold in Kazakhstan. It can get very cold in Kazakhstan. Sometimes down to -40. Theo hoped it wouldn't get that cold tonight. He was standing in the doorway of what appeared to be a shop selling the kind of lingerie that Stalin's housekeeper would have worn. The street was dark. He was waiting for his contact. After all, the fact that Kevin had been unmasked as a traitor did not mean that he was excused his duty. He felt very nervous. He was alone on his mission. Kevin could obviously not be trusted. He had to see this through on his own.

He huddled in his coat. Then he opened his plastic bag and took out a thermos flask of oxtail soup. He poured out a cup with trembling fingers. He tasted the soup. It was cold. Perhaps that was not surprising as he had made it before he left England. Three weeks before he had left England.

Two taxis had pulled up while he was waiting. They had asked if he wanted a lift and he had said 'no'. They had looked suspicious. Perhaps it was because he was wearing dark glasses at night. It must have looked odd, but you had to have a disguise otherwise you would attract attention. A third car stopped. It was another taxi, but this time a passenger got out. He was a slim, dishevelled looking man wearing a thick parka, jeans and heavy hiking boots. He paid the taxi driver, who then drove off.

Once the man had satisfied himself that the taxi had gone, he walked over to Theo. He was holding a small package in one hand. The other hand was inside his coat. He appeared to be in some pain and was walking unsteadily.

'Creosote?' said the man in heavily accented English. He seemed to have difficulty breathing.

'What?' said Theo. Then he remembered.

'Oh, yes. Creosote.'

'Well,' said the man impatiently.

'Erm yes.'

Theo fumbled around in his chaotic mind for the response.

'Yes...those bastards in the EU have banned it.'

The man seemed satisfied and gave the coded reply.

'They'll be banning brown sauce next.'

It was a moot point which of them was more afraid. Both had shaky hands. But when the other man took his hand out of his coat, Theo could see that it was covered in blood. All of a sudden, he had difficulty swallowing. His throat seemed to be blocked by something as big as a stone. The man gave him his package.

'This is big for a computer key.'

'Computer key? Are you crazy?' said the man. 'You think I would risk my life for something that could be posted out? This is a canister of nerve gas. Russian nerve gas. You must get it back to London. You must not fail!'

Theo thought his legs would buckle underneath himself.

'Do not under any circumstances try to open it. It is absolutely lethal. Do you understand?'

Theo nodded, his face white with terror.

The man looked around with an expression on his face that combined pain and panic. Two men were coming down the street. They had big coats and furry hats on.

'Go now!' he said. But Theo was stuck where he was. His legs wouldn't move.

'Who are they? KGB?'

'Who?' said the man. He seemed puzzled.

Theo remembered that Kevin had told him that the KGB did not exist anymore. But Kevin was a spy and could not be believed.

'Go! I said go!'

'Are you all right?' asked Theo in a trembly voice. 'I did first aid in the sea cadets.'

The man used his good arms to roughly manhandle Theo out of his hiding place. He literally shoved him down the street. Then suddenly, Theo regained control of his reflexes and started running. He looked behind himself only once to see the two shadowy men bearing down upon his contact. Then he was out of sight. But he heard the shots fired in the still night.

Theo ran back in utter panic towards the hotel. He made sure that he took a long and confusing route just in case he was followed. Then he realised he had confused himself and was lost. He would have to return to the shop doorway to find his path back. When he arrived, there was nobody there. It was all quiet. The three men had gone. This time he walked slowly back to Kevin's hotel.

Terror can easily turn to an irrational elation, once the danger has gone. Theo was most pleased with himself. Not since he had invented his spy detector had he felt such a sense of triumph. His blithering and dithering had been forgotten. He was completely on top of the situation.

But now he had to be careful. He entered the hotel lobby and peeped in. He could hear the American boys in the bar. As he sneaked across the lobby floor, he could see that Kevin was with them, whooping it up and shouting. He would be preoccupied for a while now. He was disgusted that a man entrusted with such a vital mission would be a drunkard. But Tregennis was a traitor. The lowest of the degenerate low. How else would traitors behave? Look at Philby and Burgess.

Theo bolted for the lift and made his way up to the room. He felt another sense of triumph. But he had some hard thinking to do. What to do with that canister? Clearly, he could not hand it over to Tregennis. It would go straight back to Moscow. Unless he was working for the Chinese. It was all complicated. He needed a plan.

Once back inside the room – Tregennis had given him the key – he sat down. He might only have a few minutes before Kevin was carried upstairs by his drinking buddies. There was only one thing for it. He must go. But where? There could only be one answer: Berlin. Theo's spiritual home. He was after all, descended from Germans. He spoke German. And Berlin was where the spies of the world congregated. Once there, it would be easier for him to make a plan. Plan later, run now. That was the plan. It was a good plan.

He bundled his bags together. Then he turned his coat inside out. He had seen that in a film. It had a tartan lining. But it looked different anyway. Then he made his way downstairs. He crossed the lobby. There were a few people there. They all stared at the man with a beard covered by a false beard, dark glasses and inside-out coat as he stepped out into the night. One of them speculated that he might be English, which explained a great deal, as they saw it.

In the bar, Kevin was still drinking and shouting. Theo could hear the raucus sound of men from the Deep South singing cockney songs.

Knees up mother Brown!

Knees up mother Brown!

Under the table you must go,

Ee-ah ee-ah ee-ah oh…

Kevin was also still fully clothed so the deranged drink-up might go on for a while yet.

CHAPTER SEVEN

Kevin woke up again with a hangover, but not as bad a hangover as the one of the previous morning. That was a bad sign. Drunks who drink constantly eventually stop getting hangovers because the alcohol never leaves their system. Gradually, over months, the Pavlovian restraint on one's own excesses is lost. He was still exhausted though – that would get worse if he didn't get a grip. The effects of drink take a heavier toll as one gets older – and he was not in the best of shape. He heaved himself out of bed and tripped over a pile of his clothes on the floor.

His tongue felt like a brush welcome mat, his eyes like frosted lenses and his brains like cold goulash. He tried desperately to clear his mind. He knew he had something important to do. It wasn't the conference, which could go to hell. It would be finishing today. He had attended the first round and he knew what to write. He was a skilled book reviewer. He knew how to assess something on the basis of minimal information. Slowly, his mind cleared. Theo! Where was Theo? He should have been back by now. Had something happened to him? Kevin felt a terrible surge of guilt. He had sent a hapless fool on an errand with which he himself had been entrusted. If any accident befell Theo, he would be responsible.

He looked at his watch. It was 10.30am. The room was a mess because he hadn't allowed the cleaners to come in. But something was missing. Theo's luggage was gone. Clearly, he had been back to the room. How had he, Kevin, managed to get back in last night? He couldn't remember if the door had been unlocked when he returned. Perhaps his drinking buddies had called the night porter and let him in.

He had to get organised. He had to get cleaned up, dressed and sort this out. He found his phone in the tangled mess on the floor and called Theo's number. No reply. That was worrying. He could try him later. But first, he needed to eat and let his body catch up with the punishment which he had given it over the past two days.

He sat on the bed and tried to muster the energy to get ready. He felt ashamed. He also had an unsettling inkling that he had called Rumana. He checked his phone. He had called her last night and the night before. What had he said? Oh, bloody hell. All the folly of his youth which had come close to ruining his life was repeating itself. He thought of phoning her again, but it would be too early in the UK. Let her sleep undisturbed. He was tormented by the certain knowledge that he had said regrettable things. But there was nothing to do but shower and go downstairs for food.

It was midday when he returned to the room. Still too early to call Rumana, but he tried Theo again and this time he got a reply.

'Theo? Where are you?'

'Somewhere you won't find me, Quisling.'

'What are you talking about? Did you meet the contact?'

'Yes, I did.'

'Did you get the computer key? I can't go home without it.'

'You liar!' shouted Theo. 'You knew there was no key. You sent me into danger. I could have been killed by the KGB.'

'There is no KGB anymore, Theo.'

'You would say that, wouldn't you? Traitor.'

'Theo, listen. Calm down. I don't know what you are talking about.'

'You knew. You knew I would be given a phial of nerve gas.'

There was a pause. Theo hadn't meant to mention that. He had betrayed one of the principal rules of being a spy: don't tell anyone very secret things, otherwise they stop being secret. But his discomfort was nothing to that of Kevin who nearly screamed in panic.

'Nerve gas!? He gave you a flask of nerve gas?'

'Yes. And I would have given it to you, so you could pass it on to your masters. But you reckoned without my spy detector.'

'Theo, listen. This is urgent. There is no spy detector. It's just a useless lump of cardboard with a bicycle lamp attached. The Cold War has been over for decades. Now you must tell me where you are.'

'You must think I'm a complete fool. Well, try and find me, Tregennis. I'm a master of disguise. I only have to turn my coat inside out and I'm invisible.'

Kevin was close to tears.

'Yes, but what will you do with the nerve gas? It's no use to you and it's dangerous.'

'Oh, yes. And you think I'll just hand it over to you, do you?'

'Theo, I am not a spy. But if you won't give it to me, hand it over to the authorities. It's no use to anyone and the government can neutralise it.'

Kevin paused. He realised that any advice he gave Theo would be useless because Theo wouldn't trust him.

Then suddenly, he could hear a noise in the background. It was a television. People speaking on TV have a different, uninterrupted rhythm from normal speech. The announcer was speaking in German. She was reading the news. Kevin, like Theo, was a German speaker.

He guessed that Theo was either on his way to, or actually in Berlin, which he thought was still a divided spy capital. He would have to follow him.

'You're right Theo. I'll never find you. You're too clever for me. But please, don't do anything stupid with that flask.'

He hung up. His phone rang immediately. It was Rumana. She didn't sound happy.

'I think you owe me an apology,' she said.

'I'm sorry. My only excuse is that I don't know what I said.'

'You were...oh, never mind. Have you started boozing again?'

'Yes, but I will stop: I have to. I've got a few problems going on at the moment.'

'Promise me you won't drink today?'

Kevin was surprised to find himself angry. Promise? What promises did he owe her? He would have promised to swim the Atlantic with a piano on his back if she would only requite his love for her. What right did she have to extract promises when she didn't care? But he said,

'It's not a question of promises. I have some real difficulties here. I might not be back for some time?'

'Oh dear. Like Captain Oates?'

'I hope so. I do hope so. Being lost in a blizzard would be a mercy right now.'

'What's happened, Kevin?'

'I can't tell you. But I might need some help from you shortly.'

'Of course. As long as it isn't illegal or immoral.'

He believed that. She was the only person he had ever met who could say that and mean it. Next, he called Fiona. She was sleepy.

'Hello darling. It's me.'

'It is I. You're supposed to be a bloody writer.'

'Yes, it is I. And I'm afraid something is up. I won't be home for a few days.'

'OK.' she said, which was better than 'good'.

'Can you take this number down?'

'What? No I can't. I'm in bed.'

'It's important.'

'Well, text it to me.'

'All right, I'll send it now. If I get any calls from that number, tell me immediately.'

'Yes. All right.'

'The number I'm sending you is a man called Theo. And if that bloke Danvers calls round, don't tell him anything.'

'OK' she said and hung up.

'Don't tell me what?' said Danvers.

Fiona snuggled up to him and said, 'You heard'.

Kevin sat on the bed and tried to make some sense.

Now just relax, he said to himself. *This is a soluble problem. A lunatic is running around Europe with a flask of deadly nerve gas and it's all your fault. There is no need to panic.*

CHAPTER EIGHT

Theo felt an ineffable thrill as he arrived in Berlin. His family had come from Germany, and Berlin was his spiritual home as a result of his calling. It was, after all, the centre of world Cold War espionage. He was, however, a little bewildered. He had expected to find the city divided and was quite shocked when he couldn't find the Berlin Wall. He asked some passers-by where Checkpoint Charlie was. They were neither British nor German. They may have been from Taiwan. They answered his questions with some bewilderment.

'Berlin Wall? Is gone.'

'Gone? Gone where?''

'Communism has fallen.'

Theo was dumbstruck.

'Communism fallen? What, while I was on the plane?'

They didn't know what he meant but they were pleased to meet a man wearing his coat inside out and wearing dark glasses. Clearly, he was blind and had nobody to dress him. They walked him to the multi-coloured, graffiti-defaced remnants of the Wall on the Niederkirchenstrasse. Theo was amazed. Where were all the Soviet troops?

'Troops? Soviet troops? Not here. Soviet gone. New world. One Germany.'

Theo hardly knew how to take this. The city had been divided when he left Kazakhstan, he was sure of that. He had seen a film once where some spies had drugged someone on a plane and kept him in suspended animation for forty years. Perhaps it was something like that.

However, when he pointed to some of the slogans painted on the remaining slabs, his guides realised that he was not blind at all. Clearly, they were the victims of some practical joke. Indeed, they suspected he might be English. They left him on his own and he wandered off to find somewhere to sit and think. Also, he needed something to eat. He found a café in a nearby street and sat glumly, wondering what to do next. The world had moved on very quickly. The Soviet Union had collapsed in a few hours and some of his skills might be obsolete in the New Order. What was the use of a spy detector if there were no spies? He idly spooned his coffee about, trying to make sense of the new situation. Theo did not like change. Few people do, especially when it comes so quickly, as it does in the modern age. All his certainties had been overturned.

On the Gold radio station at the back of the cafe, old music from the sixties made him nostalgic for the days when everything was simple. One foot over the iron curtain and nuclear Apocalypse ensued. You knew exactly where you were. None of this half-baked, colour-coded, Nancy-boy, graded escalation palaver. People had gone too soft, he mused.

In the background, Bob Dylan was droning out doom and despair in a voice fit for that and nothing else. But the rest of it was silly pop music. It was beneath Theo's serious tastes. The world was a serious place and men with a mission could only be contemptuous of the trivial trinkets of popular culture.

But, he suddenly thought, if there was no Soviet Union anymore, then what was the significance of this flask of nerve gas? Obviously, the man who had given it to him had been a spy, so the profession still existed. And if the Russians were no longer the enemy, perhaps he should just give it back. No, that couldn't be right. Otherwise, we wouldn't have had to steal it... unless – unless we were the baddies now? It was all getting very complicated in his mind. He finished his coffee and went off to find a newsagent. He needed to re-educate himself before he acted.

It was only a hunch that made Kevin think that Theo was in Berlin. He knew he was in Germany – his German was good enough to know the difference between Swiss, German and Austrian accents - but the capital was an educated guess.

The staff at the Nur-Sultan Nazarbayev International Airport had been most helpful, however, and after he had made a cash contribution to the Airport Booking Staff Benevolent Fund (no receipt necessary), they had confirmed that a man answering Theo's unique and unmistakeable description had booked a flight to Berlin. Kevin booked one too. He had plenty of expenses money left as he had hardly spent anything while in Kazakhstan. Everything at the conference and the hotel had been paid for. The only expenditure was on booze and his dubious drinking chums from The Deep South had been happy to cover that, having been paid thrice over by the entertainment value of an Englishman who couldn't hold his liquor or keep his trousers on. They would all have been earning thousands of dollars tax-free and had virtually nothing to spend it on while they were working – which was most of the time.

And so, Kevin flew to Germany. Once on the plane, he called up the Globe website on his phone. Inside in the features section was a report on the United Nations Conference in Kazakhstan. It was written 'by our correspondent in Kazakhstan, Sarah Markstein.' There was a big picture of her next to a very small picture of Astana.

I watched the UN convocation called New Horizons for Humanity with absolute amazement. I saw humanity at its best, at its most vibrant – and, most importantly, at its most optimistic.

I spent several days mixing with the brightest and the best of the whole world – and yes, that means the Third World too. I was almost dizzy with intellectual stimulation. I didn't meet anybody who wasn't brimming with ideas. I don't doubt that some people at least can see the way forward, even if we in the West have lost our way.

I bet there were imaginative initiatives, thought Kevin. I bet they've been tested with great success in Sweden.

I was told about one imaginative initiative which has been tested to great success in Sweden…

Sarah hadn't been there of course, but he could hardly blame her for filling in. Strictly speaking it was her province. Someone had to write it and the man whose job it was had gotten drunk and made a mess of it. Made a mess of everything. As usual.

He did not sleep on the plane. His body was wondering where the alcohol was and kept his mind buzzing. And he had many worries. He wasn't the only one. Theo had worries too. And so did Robert Danvers of the Secret Intelligence Service.

'This has to be kept quiet, Robert,' said his nameless superior on the other end of a secret phone line. The voice was a bit calmer now, having exhausted itself with five minutes of screeching.

'Yes sir. In my defence I must say I did not know that my contact was going to get his hands on such controversial contraband.'

'That's the whole bloody point of intelligence work. You never know what they might stumble on. It's a completely haphazard enterprise. Sometimes they might get a conference menu which tells us that someone is on a special diet and might be dying. Sometimes it's the plans for a cobalt bomb. And sometimes it's a flask of nerve gas.'

'Yes, sir.'

'Do you know how deadly this stuff is?'

'Yes sir. It could kill thousands.'

'Well, where is it then?'

'Obviously it hasn't been opened yet.'

'That's a small bloody comfort. Who is this bloke you sent to pick it up?'

'His name is...Tregennis, sir. He's normally a top-class agent. I'm sure everything's under control.'

Like all the members of his degraded profession, Danvers was a fluid liar. The nameless voice took a deep breath.

'Good. So where is it?'

'It's...in transit, I'm sure, sir.'

'Yes, well I hope so.'

There was a pause.

'There is one good thing. This nerve gas auto-neutralises after about fifteen minutes once exposed to the air.'

Danvers wondered how far he could run in fifteen minutes.

'But...' continued the voice, 'that's a small consolation for anyone living downwind.'

'Yes, sir.'

And small consolation for anybody over eighty, he thought.

'You'd better find this.'

'Yes, sir.'

The voice hung up.

Thank God he doesn't know the full truth, thought Danvers, otherwise he would be the only old Harrovian and Cambridge Boxing Blue selling the Big Issue for a living. Kevin had told Fiona and Fiona had told him that a lunatic was running around with a flask of deadly nerve gas. Danvers would need all the help he could get.

He took out a secret diary from a locked drawer. Then he took out an anonymous disposable mobile phone. He went out into the street to make the call.

A woman's voice answered and he simply said,

'Hello Otto, this is Cleo. Bank Station. One hour. Urgent. Coded red.'

Then he hung up, dismantled the phone and threw the bits into various litter bins. A suspicious policeman watched him, wondering if he might be a drug dealer. Some of them were very well dressed these days.

Clearly, the brown-haired Slavic lady who met Danvers at Bank Station was not called Otto, just as Danvers was not called Cleo.

'Hello Otto.'

'Hello Cleo.'

They walked slowly and nonchalantly down Cannon Street. They never looked at each other. She was wearing dark glasses.

'I understand an item has gone missing,' he said.

'I understand you were responsible for the abstraction.'

'Only by accident.'

'Such items do not go missing by accident. An item guarded by highly complex security arrangements would necessitate considerable expertise for its misappropriation.'

'We are as concerned as you are as to its whereabouts and are working towards its safe return.'

'Safe return? To us?'

'To any safe pair of hands.'

'That is not good enough. It belongs to us.'

'Then I am happy to tell you everything I know so that you can assist us in the search.'

'We do not recognise the system of finders-keepers. It is our property.'

'Then you must make sure that you find it. And of course, I can be assured that your people will, as usual, use all methods available without the restraints imposed upon more accountable agencies.'

Then Danvers told Otto all that he knew.

CHAPTER NINE

With Theo's number in their possession, the Russians had no trouble in tracing him to a hotel in Berlin. They arrived the next day. There were two of them. One was called Pavel, the other was called Joseph. Sometimes, when he thought it was useful, Joseph told people he had been named after Joseph Stalin. Other times, he said it was biblical. Behind his back, his subordinates, who loathed him for a useless time-server, said he was named after Goebbels. He was the smaller of the two but was the one in charge. He liked to show it by constantly contradicting every idea which Pavel suggested, even though Pavel was more experienced, more intelligent and had been trained by the Israelis.

'He's going out,' said Pavel. 'That's good. We can search his room.'

'Don't be ridiculous. Do you think he'll have it with him? I suppose you think he's put it on the bathroom shelf? He won't be an idiot, you know. He'll be a trained operative. He'll have a hiding place somewhere. We need to follow him.'

'Perhaps one of us could follow him and the other search his room?'

'Do as you are told. We must keep together. He may be armed.'

'OK,' said Pavel and shrugged.

They booked into the hotel themselves. They watched day and night. Theo went out a lot. They followed him to the shops where he bought bags of rice and pasta and cases of bottled water. He went back and forth doing this all day.

'He's up to something,' said Joseph. 'We'll have to be alert.'

Brilliant, thought Pavel, but he said,

97

'We know he's going to the shops a lot and we know roughly how long it takes. We could search the place next time he goes out.'

'Stop going on about searching the place. I'm in charge. Our job is to follow him and find out where he's hiding it.'

They followed Theo to the shops and they followed him back again. After the fifth trip, he didn't emerge again, so they kept watch on his room.

Inside, Theo decided to have a shower. He took the gas flask out of his pocket and put it on the bathroom shelf so he could watch it. When he had showered, he came out of the bathroom and tripped over a huge pile of rice bags, knocking himself out on the bedroom chair. Outside the room, Pavel and Joseph stayed ever vigilant. After a couple of hours, Pavel looked at his watch.

'Are you sure we shouldn't be doing this in shifts?'

'Be quiet.'

After another hour, the deputy manager came up in the lift and asked them with acid politeness if they had lost something.

'No, not at all,' said Pavel politely. 'We are waiting for a friend.'

'Mind your own business,' said Joseph.

'I think you had better go back to your rooms,' said the deputy manager.

'We were just going,' said Pavel politely. They both went upstairs.

'I suppose it won't do any harm to get some sleep,' said Joseph. 'I think tomorrow, we'll search his room.'

They both had a good night's sleep. In the morning, once they had got up, Joseph had wanted to go and have breakfast, but Pavel insisted that they check Theo's room. Joseph overruled him and they had a leisurely continental meal before going upstairs again. When they got there, the door was open and the cleaner was in the room. They pushed their way in. The place was empty. Theo had left.

Geoff Amis was in a miserable mood. He had been trying to contact Fiona for a few days and she was not answering his calls. He seemed a bit distant when Danvers came to visit him in his office. Amis didn't really want to meet anybody, but he had received a call from 'on high', telling him that he had to see someone from the government on an important matter of national security.

'Good of you to see me,' said Danvers, who had given his name as Thompson.

I had no choice, thought Amis, but he said,

'Not at all. Great pleasure. Always glad to co-operate with the authorities.'

He offered Danvers a seat. They looked at each other for a few seconds. Amis and Danvers were different and yet the same. They both had aquiline noses and slightly longish, silvery hair which flowed backwards – both suggestive of an aristocratic background. But Amis had been born in Catford. His accent had been developed by watching the old Jack Hawkins movies which his mother had liked. Danvers, however, had been born to it. Also, Amis was a bit shorter and had a slight stoop. This was not a problem when he was walking since it gave him an air of determination. His forward jutting aspect had the same effect as speed lines on the side of a car. But standing still, he had a slightly beaten look. Danvers, on the other hand, when standing still, looked like a statue of abstract nobility from the quad of a private school. The difference and the similarity irritated Amis.

Danvers, or Thompson, began to speak, but then hesitated, and Amis guessed that he would say it was a delicate matter, which he did.

'This is a...rather delicate matter. You have a chap here called Tregennis.'

'Oh yes,' said Amis, in a sort of 'what's-he-done-now' kind of voice.

'The truth is, he's in a bit of a sticky situation.'

Danvers-Thompson explained the facts. Or rather, he told the story in which he had asked Tregennis to do something quite simple and he, Tregennis, had gone off the rails and made a pig's ear of it.

'How can I help?' asked Amis. *This might be a good opportunity to get rid of Tregennis*, he thought. But then he thought that if he was sacked, he would be spending more time at home. And Amis thought he was still in with a chance with Fiona.

'Do you want me to pull him in?'

'Actually, no. We must keep him on the case, as it were. Bung him plenty of expenses money. I'll see that you're reimbursed.'

Amis nodded, but not necessarily in agreement. Suddenly, Tregennis was a valuable employee who couldn't really be spared. Would there be a story in all this?

'A story? There'll be a bloody huge story if you don't keep him on this. I'll make sure of that.'

Amis decided he didn't like Thompson and resolved to do him a bad turn whenever he had the opportunity. After all, he was the editor of a national newspaper, not some hired junior boot hand. But revenge is a dish that must be served cold by the weak, or those in a weak position, even though it is much more fun to pour it piping hot down the front of someone's trousers.

Danvers looked at his watch. If Amis had known that he was late for a meeting with Fiona, his vengeance would have been either volcanic or cryogenically deferred. But lethal either way.

Well, he thought eventually, what did it matter to him if Tregennis was kept out of the way? He agreed that he would do as Thompson-Danvers asked.

Danvers stood up quickly before Amis could stand up first in dismissal. They shook hands. Amis smiled at Danvers. He hated him. Danvers, for all his aloofness, was a very perceptive man. He was a skilled poker and chess player. He could tell that Amis loathed him. But Danvers didn't care if people hated him. He was that sort of person.

Later on, Danvers called Kevin.

'Hello. My name is Carruthers. You don't know me.'

'Yes I do.'

'No, I mean, you don't know my name.'

'Yes, I do. You're Danvers. The bloke who came to see me.'

There was a pause. Danvers guessed that Kevin was being deliberately ornery. He cut to the chase.

'If you want to find Theo, he's on his way to Munich in Bavaria.'

'Really? That's a worrying development – historically I mean. What's he planning to do? He's not going to start making speeches in bierkellers, is he?'

'I really have no idea. That's for you to find out. I've made arrangements for your paper to keep paying you your salary and expenses. Just find him and get that flask back. I've spoken to your boss. There won't be any publicity if we can clear this up quickly.'

'How did you track Theo?'

'Through his number of course.'

'How did you get his number? And how did you know what happened?'

'Good grief man, we're an intelligence agency. That's what we do.'

Kevin said nothing, but he was suspicious. He was surrounded by people who knew more than he did but weren't telling him anything.

CHAPTER TEN

Theo enjoyed the lovely train journey to Munich and was disappointed when he arrived. But he had work to do. He unloaded his luggage. He had a huge backpack and a trolley, plus two travel grips. He realised he had a bit too much to carry. He had seen a film once called *Rogue Male* with Peter O'Toole. (He watched a lot of films.) He thought that if he bought all his provisions locally, he would attract attention to himself, just as Peter O'Toole had done. Better by far, he had reasoned, to take everything with him. But O'Toole had had a tandem with a trailer. Now Theo realised that he was overloaded. He kept dropping stuff. People seemed to be laughing at him. The last thing he wanted was to be a spectacle. He wanted to melt into the background. His plan involved hermetic isolation. He was not a fit man, nor was he very young anymore. Also, he had been unable to find the German equivalent of All-Bran. But these obstacles and deprivations were the stuff of his mission. They were challenges to be risen to and overcome. He walked onwards and upwards with a determined stride, pausing only to pick up what he had let fall along the wayside.

Unbeknownst to him, Kevin and the two Russian men – both kept informed by their masters – followed close behind. Of course, Theo had suspected he would be followed. He had to reach his destination and hide himself soon. Meanwhile he still had his phone and could still be tracked. Of course, he didn't know this. Most of the spy films he had seen had been made before the invention of the mobile phone. However, although he was not *au fait* with gadgets that he hadn't made himself out of cardboard, he did have a plan. And it was most devilish.

Up into the high hills he walked until he came to a disused mine shaft. Whether it had ever really been a mine was a moot point. More likely, it had been a place to store equipment or stolen goods during the war. The adit was boarded up and padlocked, but the wood was rotten. There was a sign on the boarding saying:

GEFAHR DER ABSENKUNG

TRITT NICHT EIN

And then underneath

Danger of subsidence – do not enter.

He broke in with ease, throwing the sign to one side, and made his way down into the depths of the mine. Walking through passage after passage, he descended into the guts of the earth. He had prepared himself reasonably well. He had a torch and provisions for a long time. And if he slipped, well, he slipped. All would be lost, but all was lost anyway. But he had prepared well. He had a box of plasters, some kitchen roll and a tube of glue. The helpful man in the store, who had seemed to be amused by something, also sold him a box of tampons. 'Because, you never know,' he had said, tapping his nose.

Theo and the Russians followed him. Both parties realised that if Theo disappeared below ground, the signal would be lost. But they would be able to deduce that he had gone to ground somewhere. There couldn't be that many places that Theo could go.

Eventually, Theo found an open part of the mineshaft, rather like the stomach opens beneath the oesophagus. There was a shaft of light from an opening up above which provided air as well. He would be very snug here, he thought. He sat down on a small shelf and opened all his bags. He put the nerve gas flask next to himself so he could keep an eye on it.

Next, he took out a small transistor radio. There was a paper label sellotaped on it saying in Theo's spidery writing, 'spy transmitter'. Then he took out an old Post Office telephone code book from the sixties. *Telephone codes*, it said on the front. It was an old code book, but that would enable him to monitor the airwaves and relay his messages to the world. He would use the flask as a bargaining chip. The governments of the world would have to listen to him. He was finally master of his own destiny – and of the world's too. He could last here forever, thanks to his own clever preparations.

He had plenty of food to see himself through. Rice, pasta, a score of tins of this and that. He suddenly stopped and thought. Then he rummaged in his bag for a tin opener. He had all the contents of each bag all over the cave floor. But it was a fruitless search. He knew he didn't have one. He also knew that he didn't have any scissors to cut open the bags either. He tried tearing one apart and the rice went all over the floor. Not that it mattered. He didn't have any method of cooking it. He tried googling *How to cook without pans and heat*, but his phone didn't seem to be connecting. Theo's eyes narrowed with suspicion. He cast darting glances around himself. They had sabotaged his phone. This was a challenge, without a doubt. But Theo was a trained operative. None of this interfered with his master plan. He just had less time. He would have to send his demands to the United Nations and the White House by letter. He opened his wallet and took out a book of stamps. There were two left. At last, something was breaking his way. Of course, he didn't have any writing materials.

Then he came up with a brainwave. He would record the message and then send it whenever he decided that it was safe to go up to the outside world. That was a brilliant idea. No wonder he was a genius. He set his telephone on a rock with the camera pointing toward himself. He pressed the video play. Then he cleared his throat and began in his most sonorous and serious of voices.

'Governments of the world. Who I am is not important. My name is Theodore Ziegen-Wirbelsaule.'

That didn't sound right. He began again.

'My name is Theodore Ziegen-Wirbelsaule. However, my name is not important. I hold in my hand a flask of deadly nerve gas.'

He paused again. He realised that he was not holding it in his hand, so he picked it up.

'Precisely who is responsible for manufacturing this abomination I will not say. What is important is that it has fallen into my hands. Who I am is not important...'

He had said that. Never mind, he could do all the editing later.

The cave was dry and he fell into a coughing fit.

'Excuse me.'

He took a throat pastille out of his pocket and put it in his mouth.

'Ah, that's better.'

He held up the packet to the camera.

'I recommend Hall's Mentholyptus for a sore throat, although I prefer the taste of Tunes Cherry menthol. That's just a little feedback for the cough sweet industry which may be useful. I would also like it if they sold them in little bags like Fisherman's Friends. But that's just my opinion and it has nothing to do with any of my demands. Now back to this flask. My conditions are as follows: Number One, the complete renunciation of all chemical and biological weapons by all the leaders of the world – and no cheating. Secondly, a world convocation headed by me...'

He thought for a moment. Style was everything.

'...headed by myself, dedicated to the eradication of nuclear weapons and the beginning of a New Era of World Peace. Now I know you will say that atomic weapons have kept the peace for many years. I have considered that...'

Theo had indeed considered that they might say that. What he hadn't considered was a response to it. He thought of himself as an idealist. Like all idealists he looked at the world in a very simplistic way.

'I will come back to that.'

He pondered for a moment. Then a thought came to him; something which had been bothering him for a long time.

'By the way, I think it would be very helpful if all cheese and onion crisps could be sold in blue packets. It is ridiculous and confusing to put them in both green and blue. Again, this is just a suggestion and does not constitute one of my demands.'

Well, fair's fair, you couldn't hold the world to ransom over the colour of crisp packets. He was not a complete lunatic.

Suddenly, Theo looked at the phone on the rock. It had gone blank. He picked it up and checked it. It had switched itself off. After a while, he realised that it needed charging and there was nowhere to charge it. That could be a major setback to his stratagem. He needed a new plan. Every time he started a plan, he found that ten minutes later he needed a new one. It was most annoying. But it kept him on his mettle.

The Russians reached the cave before Kevin. This was hardly surprising, as they were younger and fitter. Kevin kept having to stop and drink water or have a cigarette. He found it difficult enough to keep going this distance on the flat. Pavel and Joseph had been told that there was no tracking signal on Theo's mobile anymore. But that was not a problem, since it confirmed that they had trailed their quarry to his destination.

'See, I told you,' said Joseph. But Pavel had no idea what Joseph was supposed to have told him.

'What do we do now?' he asked. He knew very well what they had to do but if he suggested it, Joseph would deliberately suggest something else.

'Well, first,' said his boss, 'we have a rest.'

Pavel felt OK. He was a highly trained operative. He knew that while rest was important, it was just as important, if you weren't exhausted, to keep up the pressure on your quarry while you had him. And besides, the Western agencies would be coming after Theo as well. If they were found armed on NATO territory, there would be a serious diplomatic incident. They had to get that flask first. He was amazed that Joseph couldn't see that.

'He's not going anywhere, Pavel.'

'We don't know that. There might be another exit.'

'Nonsense,' said Joseph, which word was his answer to many a difficult suggestion. He sat down and took out a sandwich and a bottle of orangeade from the pockets of his heavy camouflaged flak jacket. He had bought the jacket in Berlin. He thought it made him look the business.

It was a dangerous situation and both men had guns. Pavel was for going straight in there and getting the flask back. But Joseph liked to think of himself as a cautious intellectual. Well, thought Pavel, they must have made him an officer for some reason, so he shrugged and sat down. If he was thinking that Joseph might be a coward, he did not say so. It started to get dark and cold.

Down in the Hadean gloom of the cave at night, Theo slept, clutching the deadly flask to his body like a baby. He was exhausted and had been on the go for quite a while.

Sitting outside the cave, both of the Russians must have dozed a little. But Pavel suddenly jerked awake.

'Joseph! Listen! Someone's coming!'

Pavel had his gun out quickly.

'Put that away!' shouted his boss. 'I'll say when there's shooting to be done.'

Pavel obeyed. But he knew that he had been right. They should have gone in immediately. These caves probably went on for miles. And Theo might be lost forever down in the tenebrous convolutions. Or he might have escaped through another opening.

They both listened. They could hear the heavy tread of an overweight man who would have been exhausted carrying the Sunday newspapers. He was breathing like a flasher and swearing as he caught his clumsy feet on the rocks, weeds and tussocks along the way.

'Come on,' Joseph shouted in a hoarse whisper.

They both rose and ran into the adit of the cave. It was completely dark now and they moved in a farcical kind of slow-motion panic. Pavel had thought to bring a box of matches and for a mercy Joseph didn't tell him to put them away. They inched along. Pavel could hear Joseph whimpering like a puppy behind him.

Inevitably, they managed to find the clearing. Theo was asleep, but leapt up in terror when he heard them. He shouted, 'You'll never take me alive!'

Joseph started and nervously fired his gun into the air. All three were frozen as the bullet ricocheted around. Then they heard the rumblings of a threatening rock fall. Theo stood rooted to the spot. The two Russians moved backwards.

'Let's get the hell out of here,' said Pavel, and for once his boss didn't argue. As they hurried in an undignified panic back towards the entrance, they heard the entire cave roof fall upon the poor lunatic. They made it to the entrance of the cave and stopped to regain their breath, stolen by terror.

'We'd better get down to civilisation,' said Joseph, who just wanted to run away. But Pavel stopped him.

'There's no hurry. We've got a quarter of an hour. If that nerve gas flask is broken and the gas gets out then there is nowhere to run to. We might just as well wait for fifteen minutes. If nothing happens, then the flask was buried unopened or the gas was trapped under the rock fall.'

Even in the dark, he could see his boss go white. Joseph sat down in silence. Pavel sat down beside him.

'I never wanted to do this job,' said Joseph after a while in a shaky voice.

Pavel wasn't really interested in Joseph's life. His blind panic and cravenness had just caused an accident which might have killed hundreds of thousands of innocent people. In any case, Pavel hadn't wanted to join the Russian intelligence services either. But there were no other jobs out in the wilds of Siberia. He had his own problems. They would both be held accountable for this. And Joseph might tell some appalling pack of lies which he would have to support. Or he might blame Pavel.

'I was always more artistic,' Joseph continued.

'Yeah.'

'I'm a good artist. Not brilliant, but I could have been a designer. You know that big sculpture in the middle of Moscow, the one representing the fall of the Soviet Union?'

'Oh, yes,' said Pavel, suddenly interested.

'I could have designed that.'

Pavel wondered whether his future would be any worse if he shot Joseph through the head and threw him down the mine. He suspected that there would be a cover up of this affair anyway and that all the nations of the world would conspire to keep it quiet, so he would probably be no worse off. They waited and waited as both their watches seemed to have stopped telling the time. Eventually, the fifteen minutes passed. They gave it another ten and then left to go down to the nearest village.

'Well, I think we can congratulate ourselves on a job well done,' said Joseph, who was now in a much brighter mood. 'Come on, let's go home.'

They both started walking.

'Perhaps I'll show you some of my sketches,' he said.

CHAPTER ELEVEN

Once the Two Stooges had left the area, Kevin appeared. He had heard them talking in the dark and had bided his time. Clearly, there was no danger anymore. He was exhausted and he was not going down into the cave until it was light. But he couldn't go back down to the town and then return as his heart would not stand the strain. So, he sat down, huddled up in his coat and settled into the alcove of a sort of craggy rock protuberance. It was chilly but not freezing. He slept as best he could, (which, to be perfectly honest, was not much worse than he normally slept these days).

Morning came and displayed a beautiful view of the surrounding mountainous countryside. But Kevin had other concerns. He went into the cave and felt his way down to the clearing which was now a pile of rubble. He could see Theo, half buried in the shower of stones and rocks. Somewhere inside that rock pile was the flask. If it was broken, it was neutralised. If it was not broken, then it was hidden completely and was safe until somebody tried to dig it out. He looked with pity upon poor Theo. Then he felt his neck pulse. Nothing. He was quite dead.

'Oh, you poor fool,' he said, partly to himself and partly to Theo. 'I did this to you. I'm sorry.'

He decided that a speech was in order.

'You and I are one of a kind, Theo. The last of a dying breed. Men of integrity and dignity. The Old School. You died for a myth, but you believed that myth and died in good faith for it. And that makes us the same, Theo. We are men of honesty and good intent.'

After a respectful pause, he leaned over and stole Theo's wallet out of his pocket.

'Hope you don't mind, but I need this. I'd get it back to you, but you don't need it. When I'm in a better position, I'll make a donation of the same amount to some charity. Did you support any particular charity, Theo? Any cause that was close to your heart?'

But Theo was silent and just stared at the cave roof.

Kevin also helped himself to the false beard and dark glasses which Theo had been carrying. Souvenirs of a life dedicated to a madness. Just like everyone else. His, though, had been a different kind of madness. He had created a unique world and died for it.

Kevin realised with shame that he didn't know any prayers, so he sang a hymn – or at least as much as he could remember of *All Things Bright and Beautiful* - in his shaky karaoke voice. As much as he could remember was the first four lines. Then he left the cave and made his way to…somewhere else. All he knew about his next destination was that it would be less far up.

He eventually found himself in a village called Schlamberg. Once he had booked a room in a quiet hostel, he called Fiona. He told her that the danger was over. Fiona told Danvers and Danvers spoke to Otto and Amis. He called Amis at home, which Amis did not appreciate.

'Mr Amis, I trust you're well this evening?'

'Very well indeed, Mr Thompson. How are you?' said Amis, with towering insincerity.

'Yes, well thanks. Now regarding the delicate matter which we discussed.'

'Oh yes.'

'I have some good news.'

You've got a terminal illness, thought Amis. But he said,

'That's great. I like good news. Of course, as a newspaper man I prefer bad news. It's better from a professional point of view.'

They both gave a forced laugh.

'Well, I think I can promise you a good story that you wanted. Good news and bad news.'

'That's the best kind of story. The King is dead, long live the king. That's the motto of the news service.'

Danvers sighed. *What a tiresome little man,* he thought.

'Now, if you remember, I told you that we had to keep this thing with Tregennis under wraps.

'Yeeessss.'

'Well, I'm happy to say the situation has changed. I think it's now in our interest to give him a taste of celebrity.'

Amis was suspicious.

'Will he like this taste of stardom?'

'I don't think so. But whether he does or doesn't, it won't last. Fame these days is a very ephemeral phenomenon, don't you find?'

'It won't last?'

'No – unless he achieves immortality through an early death.'

'I don't think he can have an early death. He's over fifty.'

Danvers sighed. Some people were so literal.

'Can you be more specific about what kind of fame he will achieve?'

'Notoriety, Geoffrey. Notoriety is the word.'

And he explained the situation.

After a good night's sleep at the hostel, which had been preceded by a good day's sleep, Kevin woke up feeling exhausted. That was partly because of his exhausting climb and partly because his bed and pillow had obviously been filled from the local mountain scree. After his usual morning ablutions, he went down to find something to eat. On the small reception desk near the stairs was a pile of newspapers. The headline of all of them was pretty much the same.

HABEN SIE DIESEN MANN GESEHEN?

Underneath the bold rubric, where Kevin had expected to see a picture of Theo, was a picture of himself. The story basically said that he was a missing journalist who had run off with a flask containing a dangerous nerve gas, which had been stolen from a laboratory. The country of origin was not mentioned. There was nobody at the desk, so Kevin turned round and walked very briskly upstairs.

When he came back down in about half an hour, he was wearing a pair of dark glasses and a false beard. He also had his coat turned inside out. As he walked out of the door, he heard a man sitting in the lounge say, 'Englander'.

Meanwhile, back in their own hotel room, Joseph showed Pavel picture after picture of his drawings and art works. Each time he swiped them on his phone, Pavel said, 'Yeah…yeah…yeah.' Did he have to fall asleep with indifference or scream with exasperation before Joseph realised that he wasn't interested?

116

The day wore on. Joseph had many pictures.

CHAPTER TWELVE

Kevin had a brilliant plan. The specifics of it were cunning to the point of genius. He would get on a bus or a train and see where he ended up. After that, he would wing it for a bit. The brilliance of the plan was that if *he* didn't know where he was going, then nobody else would. It was a plan he had been living all his life. Tried and tested to perfection. Tried and tested to destruction.

The first bus that came was going directly into Munich. This was a good sign. He had two reasons for being pleased that he was going to a large city. Firstly, he could get lost in the crowds. People minded their business more in big places. Secondly, he wanted to find a phone shop. He had plenty of money, thanks to Amis, Theo and Danvers. Of course, he wouldn't be able to charge a new phone in time – and it might look suspicious to ask the shop to do it - but he could swap the SIM into his old one. The first thing would be to draw out as much cash as he could, as they might be able to freeze his bank account.

He wandered around the city for a while until he found a Vodafone store on the Marienplatz. It was a sizeable place, which was what he wanted. The staff were all very young, as he had expected. This was good too. Young people didn't tend to read newspapers so much these days and what news they got on their phones and tablets tended to be very selective. It was certainly a risk though but one he had to take. One salutary thing was that his German was very good, good enough not to necessarily give him away as an Englishman. And in any case, who would expect an Englishman to speak a foreign language? It was the perfect cover. Next, he needed a base where he could think and plan his next steps.

• * * *

'Kevin? Where are you? What on earth are you up to?'

'Rumana, I'm in serious trouble.'

'I know you are. They're saying you stole some nerve gas and ran off with it.'

'I didn't do anything of the sort. Of course I didn't. What would I want with a flask of nerve gas?'

'Well, that's what they're saying. You aren't drunk, are you?'

'No, I'm not. I swear I'll never drink again.'

'I'm glad to hear it. I'm not sure I've forgiven you for the last time.'

'Why? All I did was say I loved you.'

'And you kept texting me saying, *Rumana, Rumana, be my banana.*'

'I meant every word of it. I do love you.'

'Kevin, you must stop this. I'm getting married soon.'

'Oh, look we can't discuss this now. I'm in a terrible jam. You're the only one I can go to.'

'Kevin, you're a fifty-year-old reporter. I can't possibly be the only person you know.'

'No. I know lots of people; but you're the only one I can trust. You're the only person I know who's honest. Rumana, it's a matter of life and death.'

There was a pause. Kevin wondered if she was asking herself if his life and death were worth getting agitated about. Eventually, she said,

119

'You don't have this thing really. Do you? Truthfully?'

'No, I swear it. And anyway, it's neutralised now. And what's more, they know it is. I don't know why they've done this to me. I'm completely innocent.'

'What do you want me to do?'

'When I was on the crime beat, I used to know a man who forged passports.'

'Kevin, you must be joking. I'm not getting involved in that.'

'I'm not asking you to do anything illegal. I just want you to go to my wife and get some passport photos. She'll give them to you.'

'Why can't your wife do it?'

'She wouldn't. She's not wonderful like you.'

'They'll catch you just as easily in Europe.'

'No, they won't. I can go anywhere in Europe without a passport. But I want to come home. At some time, anyway. I can't use my own passport. I want to make sure I can prove my innocence before they catch me. Please help me.'

'Oh, all right.'

'Oh, my darling!'

'Try to control yourself Kevin. And take care.'

'I'll try.'

He gave her his address and she made a note of it. It wasn't that she didn't want to help him, but she just knew they would catch him eventually. She didn't really want to get into trouble over a lost cause. But there again, much as she would never love him, he *was* a friend and she *was* fond of him.

She went downstairs to the car park under the building and drove off to the suburbs. When she arrived outside Kevin's house, she parked up. A large, expensive car had also pulled up outside the house and a very handsome and sophisticated-looking man got out. He went to Fiona's house. Fiona came out as though she had been expecting him. (Rumana had met Fiona before at the Christmas party.) They kissed and then both got into the car. Rumana took a photo of them from her phone. Then she decided to try to follow them, if it wasn't too far.

It wasn't. They went to a local wine bar called the Pirate's Chest. There was a picture of a buxom female pirate outside. Rumana parked again and waited until they were inside. If Fiona recognised her, she would simply pretend it was a coincidence.

Rumana sat at a table and ordered a coke. The couple were too far away for her to hear their conversation, but she wanted to do two things. Firstly, she wanted to see if they were really lovers, which their behaviour together at the table confirmed. And secondly, to get a good look at the man. There was an air of importance about him. He was very well dressed and urbane in his movements. Then she went back to the office and called Kevin after sending him the photo.

'That's Danvers!' shouted Kevin. 'The bastards! I'll kill them both.'

'Calm down, Kevin. There's nothing you can do. You have more important things to worry about.'

Rumana didn't bother to point out that Kevin would have gladly betrayed his wife if she, Rumana, had been available or willing.

'Did you get the photos?'

'Well, of course I didn't. There's no point now. Anything your wife knows will go straight back to him. They'd be waiting for you if you came back.'

'What can I do?'

Kevin was almost weeping.

'Oh, good grief Kevin, I don't know! I suppose you'll just have to try and lie low for a while. I'm assuming that you aren't considering giving yourself up and explaining your behaviour.'

'Perhaps I will later, but at the moment, I just wouldn't know how to begin.'

He hung up. He felt awful. He was a wanted and hunted man. His wife had betrayed him. The woman he loved did not want him. He had no job, and limited resources and he was far away from home, if he had a home. He was stranded in Europe. He was a lonely cork bobbing on a dark, cold, turbulent ocean. However, on the credit side of the ledger, he could now put, *Familiar with many exotic destinations* on his CV.

Kevin's first task was to find a photo booth. He needed passport photos. This was a fairly easy thing to organise. Then he needed to go to the post office and send them to Rumana. Both these courses involved being seen in public places and hoping that the other customers had not studied the press that morning. The second challenge was to find somewhere to stay without arousing attention. Then he came up with a brainwave. He would take an overnight train to somewhere. Paris maybe – or maybe even further. One step at a time. He would need to grow a beard. Not the most sophisticated idea in the litany of camouflage brainwaves, but enough for now.

•   *   *   *

Pavel took the plane back to Moscow on his own. It was very sad about Joseph getting shot like that. Of course, he had died a noble death in the line of duty and that was no waste. Pavel would make sure in his report that Joseph had a full and proper tribute followed by a hero's funeral. The report would have to be written with great subtlety so that all who read it deduced, without being told, that Joseph had shot himself while cleaning his gun.

'Of course, we understand, Sergeant Kirgov. You wish to protect your superior officer's reputation. Your loyalty to your friend and colleague does you great credit. But you must tell us the truth about what happened.'

'Yes sir, it's just that he deserved so much more from life than such an undignified end.'

'Yes. I know this is difficult for you but...I must ask...was he suffering from depression at all...?'

'Depression? Well...I'm not a doctor, but I will say he hadn't been exactly in good spirits recently...but...no, no...I can't believe that he shot himself, sir. A man like that? I won't believe it.'

Pavel would personally offer to speak to his family. He would not go so far as to suggest a medal, although a great service had been done for the FSB in removing Joseph from active duty in such a decisive way.

CHAPTER THIRTEEN

It took three days for Rumana to get the photos in the post. She had hoped that they would never come. She was not looking forward to helping Kevin. Of course, she liked him. Not in that way, but she liked him. And she felt sorry for him. Also, she was certain that he was innocent of the appalling crime of which the intemperate newspaper headlines accused him. But weighed in the other balance was her incorruptible honesty.

She pulled up outside a shabby looking house in a not-too-salubrious area of London. The house was a three-storey terrace, split up into flats. She went to the front door and pressed the top buzzer. A voice distorted by a cheap, decades-old intercom told her to come up. She walked unsteadily up the unlit and creaky stairs covered by the shreds of an old carpet. She knocked and a short, grubby man in his fifties opened the flat door.

'The bell doesn't work,' he said, in a voice which was actually very similar to the voice she had heard downstairs through the intercom. Now she really wished she hadn't come. The man she had come to see – an old crime-beat acquaintance of Kevin's – was called Remington. Rumana didn't think that was his real name. He had probably had many of them.

'My name is Rumana Hamid,' she said. Then it occurred to her that she shouldn't have given her name – at least not her real one – but she had no previous training in subterfuge.

'I've come on behalf of a Mr Smith.'

'Eh?'

'Mr Smith.'

'Oh, you mean Kevin Tregennis! Works for the Globe. Yes, of course. Come in.'

'Yes, that's right,' she said, before the man could tell the world Kevin's address, height and star sign.

'Come in,' he said again.

She wasn't sure if she really wanted to, but he moved away from the door and back into the gloom of his apartment, so she had to. The state of the flat was a living contradiction of Quentin Crisp's assertion that if you never clean your flat, after two years the dirt doesn't get any higher. There were a few sticks of furniture here and there. The odd chair and a table. But mainly the flat was full of newspapers. There were newspapers everywhere. On the furniture, tied up in bundles, lying on the floor, opened and with bits and pieces cut out. The papers obviously went back years. He must have had a hell of a scrap book somewhere. She looked around in amazement. He must have noticed it.

'I like to keep up with current events,' he said by way of explanation. Then he erupted into a fit of coughing straight out of a Dickensian workhouse. After his face had changed through the several colours of a lobster, resting finally on pink, he took a deep breath. Then he lit a thick, exotic-looking cigarette, apparently filled with the sweepings from the floor of a ropemaking factory. He savoured it for a few seconds. Then he got down to business.

'What can I do for you, Miss Hamid?'

'I've got some photos.'

'Ah yes,' said the man. He looked at the photos, shook his head and clicked his tongue.

'He's a bit out of date, your friend. The world has moved on from cardboard blue passports. You can't just stick a photo in with a tube of glue anymore. They're complicated now. Optical stuff. Computers. Biometrics and all that jimmy-jam. Difficult. Takes a bit of time. Well, a lot of time.'

Although by no means unintelligent, Rumana was not enough of a woman of the world to know that this uncertainty was part of the haggling process.

'Oh, is that going to be a problem?'

Remington told her how much she could expect to pay. It wasn't her money of course, and Kevin had transferred more than enough. But she was shocked on his behalf.

'Well, I suppose it will have to be,' she said. And in accordance with the traditions of greedy chancers, Remington cursed himself for not asking for more. The financial shock caused him to suffer another bronchial eruption that rattled the windows. Rumana was surprised that they didn't fall out. She was also surprised that he was still alive at the end of it. She wanted this interview over as soon as possible, so she offered him some cash, but he refused it.

'Give him these bank details and then burn them. Tell him to transfer the money. Half now, half later. You can pick it up in a few days.'

'I'll transfer it myself,' she said.

There was a pause, and she took this as a sign that she could take her blessed leave. She thanked him and felt her way down the stairs,

126

wishing she had worn trainers instead of heels. Once out in the street she took a deep breath of fresh air. She felt as though she had swum the Ganges. Even from down there, she could hear him coughing again. Rumana decided to ask her father for some advice. She was very near to where he worked. She drove down to Hamid's General Store and parked outside. It worried her that it was always easy to park outside his shop. Mo Hamid's store was on the main road out of London, through Walthamstow.

You don't see many outlets like Hamid's anymore. It sold everything. The logistics were agonising. As a general rule, the mature and discerning entrepreneur deals in sizeable products - houses, industrial machinery and armaments for example – where the sale of only one item turns in a tangibly handsome profit. (And the suckers downstream could deal with the spare parts and customer support.) Mo was right at the nether end of the commercial taxonomy along with the tobacconists and newsagents of old, tearing his hair out at the challenge of staying on top of the flow of goods in and out of his erratic business. He was in what was known as the fast-moving consumer goods industry. That was the theory, but the products themselves could only move quickly if the customers did. Mo's customers – on the increasingly rare occasions when they showed up - were deliberative and unexcitable, with the exception of the shoplifters, who displayed sprite-like suppleness and ingenuity.

Even worse, today was the six-monthly stock take. The age of the silicon chip and computer programmes notwithstanding, it was a long, agonising march down to insanity. Sometimes, at this time of year, he

127

awoke from grim dreams in which he was trapped in a mad whirling maelstrom of Mars Bars, screwdrivers, screws, ball point pens, pocket-sized tissues, balloons, joss sticks and nail clippers. Every item he sold was a locust in a thick cloud of confusion, nibbling at the greenery of his spiritual well-being, mouthful by tiny mouthful. It was a hard life.

Only the thought of retirement kept him compos mentis. In two years, he would be able to collect his private pension. The children were grown up and, according to tradition, it would soon be their turn to look after him and Mrs Hamid. And now, here was Rumana, looking troubled. Much as he cherished his daughter, this was not a welcome interruption.

'Hello Dad.'

'Hello. What brings you here?'

'I haven't stopped by for a while. Is everything OK?'

'Yes. Why?'

'Erm...you know. I just wondered.'

'Is anything wrong with you?'

'Well, I did want to ask you something. The answer to your first question is, No, I'm not in any trouble. But a friend of mine is. And the answer to your second question is, No, that isn't the agony aunt type of friend as in 'My friend may be pregnant.''

Mo stared at his daughter for a while and then turned to stare at the computer screen on the counter.

'I need to order some more grout,' he said finally.

'It's this man Kevin Tregennis... You know. The one you've seen on telly. Erm...I used to work with him. He's erm...Well, he's a friend really...and he's in a bit of trouble and I don't really know how to help him... You know...Kevin. The one on the telly...'

After a moment's thought, her father spoke.

'Friendship is very important in life, my darling. It's your solemn duty as his friend to say to him, "Sort out your own problems and leave me alone." Believe me, he'll thank you for it.'

'Why would he thank me?'

'Polyfilla,' he said. 'I need more Polyfilla.'

'Dad, he's in a lot of trouble.'

He looked up briefly and then went back to his stock take.

'You'd better ask your mother. She normally deals with trouble.'

'Yes. Yes, I'll do that.'

Rumana left the shop and drove to the family house. The Hamid's residence was around the corner, one of a million three-storey terraces in London, but one of the very few which had not been converted into three flats. It worried Rumana that it was harder to park outside the family home than outside her dad's shop.

Rumana's mother was a semi-retired agency teacher, so it was likely that she would be at home. Mrs Hamid was getting coffee and cakes ready. That meant she was expecting guests, which was her default social activity. The best crockery was on the table.

'I'm expecting some friends,' said Mrs Hamid as Rumana walked into the living room. Unlike her husband, she had almost lost her foreign accent.

'Anyone I know?'

'No, but they have a son your age.'

'But you've already found someone for me!'

'There's nothing wrong with having a back-up plan. You should always be ready for any of life's exigencies. Anyway, he wants a job in a shop.'

'Can we afford to take anyone on? Do we need anyone?'

'No, but that's not the point. Are you all right, dear? You look bothered.'

'Father said you're better with trouble.'

'I'm nothing of the kind, but he's better at passing it on to others. What is it?'

'A friend of mine...don't look like that, it isn't me, it *is* a friend of mine...He's a bit accident prone. A fool. He's older than I am but he never learns. Gets himself into all sorts of trouble.'

Mrs Hamid looked suspicious.

'Is this your father we're talking about?'

'No, it's someone I work with.'

Rumana's mother offered her coffee and cake. She accepted the former but not the latter, which was the correct response.

'And what did your father say?

'He said he needed more Polyfilla.'

'I see. Well, if that's what he said, I'm sure he knows what he's talking about.'

'You've never said that about him before.'

'Oh no. Under normal circumstances, he doesn't. But he's pretty good with things like Polyfilla. I'm sure he wouldn't make a mistake about something like that.'

Rumana decided to come to the point.

'Have you ever broken the law or done something wrong to help a friend?'

'No. Never. And no true friend would expect you to. You must tell him to sort out his own problems.'

'That's what father said.'

'Of course. That's what I tell him. It was my idea.'

'Thanks mum.'

Rumana finished her coffee and left before she was forced to meet another prospective husband.

Meanwhile, Kevin was winging his way through the night to France, desperately willing his beard to grow. He was smiling for the first time in ages. He had another plan. And this one was truly inspired.

CHAPTER FOURTEEN

France has the distinction of being the only place outside New York where the terms 'intellectual' and 'pseudo-intellectual' are co-terminous and indistinguishable. Many of these people can be seen at Le Marais. The Le Marais district is the Covent Garden of Paris. It is an affluent and fashionable area in the 4th Arondissement, full of trendy boutiques, independent galleries and cafes. It is also Paris's favourite spot for street artists.

The artist who was attracting the most attention at the moment was an Australian called Kelvin Trelawny. Kelvin's act was entitled *The Spy Detector*. Dressed in a raincoat which was turned inside out, plus false beard over a real beard and dark glasses, Kelvin used the instrumentality of a cardboard spy detector to identify treachery and hypocrisy in his bourgeois audiences. At least, that is what the blurb on his leaflet said. Trelawny said very little but used the medium of mime to condemn the outrages of modern industrial society and its warmongering elites, it continued. Trelawny's mime act was accompanied by a ghetto blaster which combined cacophonous concrete music with the sounds of the urban maelstrom and modern warfare, apparently. After several days of this, he had acquired enough of a following to attract the interest of artistic talent-spotters.

Trelawny appeared on a French arts programme called *L'Art Signifie*. He was, as usual, sitting with his back to the camera, as he did not think that artists should be famous or well known. There are artists who are anonymous, he explained to the interviewer, and there are the traitors to art. The interviewer was filmed afterwards nodding thoughtfully.

132

Rumana was reading the write-up on the internet when she got a call from the great artist himself.

'Hello Rumana, it's me.'

'Who's me?'

'I am.'

'Oh, hello Kevin. Are you all right?'

'Did you get it?'

'Yes. I've had it for ages. I was expecting you to call.'

'Did you pay him?'

'Of course, otherwise he wouldn't have given it to me. Are you coming back then?'

'I can't really until I get the passport.'

'Well, how are you going to do that?'

'Don't worry. You'll have to bring it.'

'I'm not bringing it. This has gone far enough, Kev…this has gone far enough. Why don't you just give yourself up to a lawyer and tell them what happened?'

'Oh, no you don't. Have you ever heard of the Matrix Churchill Affair?'

'Vaguely,' she said, which meant, of course, that she hadn't.

'Look it up. It's what happened to a British businessman who risked his life to spy for his country. They stitched him up and then he went to court for sanctions busting in Iraq. MI6 tried to hang him out to dry but the case collapsed.'

'Well, there we are then. Justice and the truth came out,' she said, not even convincing herself.

'But,' she continued. 'I can't possibly take the time off to come over and give it to you.'

'Aah, but you can. You're the arts correspondent, aren't you?'

'No, I'm the fashion correspondent on an arts magazine.'

'Exactly. Now if you study the press, you'll find that Kelvin Trelawny is very reluctant to give interviews because it demeans his art. But you're going to get a scoop interview with me. Clever, eh?'

'Oh, brilliant. I wish I'd never met you.'

'I'll send you my details. See if your editor wears it.'

'My editor will wear anything. And she often does.'

CHAPTER FIFTEEN

Rumana had managed to get the permission of her editor to go to Paris. The only problem had been that the arts correspondent, Mireille, who was French, thought that it was *her* job. There was a bit of an argument in the editor's office, which could barely hold three people, especially not in a hostile environment. Rumana tried to explain that Trelawny would not talk to anyone else.

'Why? Why not? What is so special about you?' demanded Mireille. 'I shall speak to the Union.'

'What union? There is no union,' said Jemima, the editor.

Eventually, it was agreed that Rumana would do the interview, but that Mireille would write it and by-line it. This meant that Mireille was denied an all-expenses trip to her home city, but there was nothing she could do. Jemima said she had a lunch and drew the argument to a close.

By some preternatural miracle, the French air traffic controllers were again not on strike and Rumana arrived in Paris promptly at lunchtime the next day, only to be held up for two hours by a baggage handlers dispute. Once this was resolved, she got a taxi – the drivers having just agreed to a settlement and returned to work that morning – and was soon at a good hotel which boasted that it had not seen a staff walk-out for several weeks.

After unpacking, she made her way to the Le Marais, where Kelvin Trelawny was holding court. He was pointing the cardboard contraption at members of the audience and saying either *Spy! Traitor!* Or *Conformist!* The crowd which had gathered around him applauded. After Kevin had passed around the hat and they had dispersed,

Rumana took him to a small café round the corner. Once they had sat down, she tried to take a snap of him.

'No photos please,' he said to her. 'They rob the artist of dignity. He becomes a wanted man. A poster on a wall. A fugitive from his own identity and from his own destiny. His soul is stolen, as the Arabs once believed.'

'Don't overdo it,' said Rumana.

'Good grief! Can't you see that overdoing it is the essence of the whole thing?'

She turned on her little Dictaphone and began the interview.

'Who is the Spy Detector?'

Kevin began his well-practised spiel with forceful passion.

'The Spy Detector must be nobody – but he must be everybody. One of the crowd, but anonymous. But also, he must stand out. He must be Albert Camus' metaphysical rebel. A man who refuses to be moved - and yet a fugitive. An exile.'

Kevin accompanied these pronouncements with ecstatic and erratic hand gestures as though he were manipulating invisible hand puppets. He seemed to be living the part, thought Rumana. She nodded and smiled as if dealing with a lunatic. Perhaps she was.

'Interesting. I notice that you have chosen to make your spiritual home in France. Which French artists have most influenced you?'

'Mainly Alain Robbe-Grillet. Just as he was an anti-novelist, so I must be the anti-artist.'

'He's ancient. What about modern artists?'

'Art is dead.'

'And this is why you wear a false beard over your real beard. Because you are the anti-artist?'

'Exactly.'

After she had finished her questions, Rumana took him to a good restaurant for an expenses-paid dinner. Kevin felt a bit shabby, which was all to the good for his cover but all to the bad as he wanted to impress her. He wanted to be seen at his best, something which he hadn't been for a couple of weeks.

Needless to say, he had been feeling a bit down recently, but the sight of Rumana had perked him up considerably.

'So, what are you going to do now, Kevin?'

'Well, I'll hang on here for a bit.'

'But you can't. They'll unmask you eventually. Anyway, what was the whole point of my bringing you a passport if you want to stay here?'

'I don't know. I'll come back soon but this is the first time in years that I've been having any fun.'

He giggled and Rumana thought that he didn't look well. He had lost weight and she couldn't work out whether that was a bad thing or a good thing at his age. Yes, he had needed to lose weight, but he looked sallow and haggard.

'I still think it would be better if you just came clean and told the authorities the truth.'

'Impossible. They'd just deny everything. I'd just sound like one of those loonies who believes he works for the secret services.'

'Like poor Theo.'

'Yes. Poor Theo.'

They were silent for a few seconds.

'Well, I'll get the bill,' she said. And then, naïve as ever, she invited him back to her room for coffee. He accepted her offer of having a shower. And then, with bath towel around him, he tried it on with her. She had been sitting on the bed, waiting for him to finish. He sat down next to her and put his arm around her.

'Oh, Rumana! You don't know how much I need you.'

'No, Kevin. I've told you, I'm engaged. Not that I would do that anyway.'

'Oh, darling,' he said, falling down backwards onto the bed in defeat. 'You're so wonderful. I love you so much. You're so…good.'

'Yes, Kevin. That's why I won't sleep with you.'

Kevin left and returned to his own little room; Rumana returned to London.

Kevin was not worried about anyone seeing him in the arts magazines or on the arts programmes. Very few people read them or watched them. In fact, he could only think of one person who read the *Art and Stuff* magazine which Rumana worked for. His wife, Fiona.

'Bloody hell!' said Fiona, as she leafed through her latest copy. 'That's Kevin!'

'Why so it is!' said Danvers, sitting next to her on the sofa. She was virtually living at Danvers' place now. She wanted to stay away from her own place as Amis had kept coming round.

'So it is,' he said.

CHAPTER SIXTEEN

The French police came for Kevin at dawn, the next day. He was just leaving the little pension, which was his digs, when they swooped. There were some press reporters there, but suddenly Kelvin Trelawny was not reluctant to be photographed.

'Monsieur Kevin Tregennis?'

'No; I have no permanent identity.'

'Very convenient, I'm sure. You are under arrest.'

'For what?' asked Kevin, declaiming to the reporters. 'For challenging the status quo? For asking the pertinent questions? For daring to go where no other artist dare? Yes, I am guilty of that.'

Two of the reporters applauded him as the police pushed him down into their car.

At the police station, he was processed and then taken to an interview room where he was interrogated by a detective in his late thirties called Casson, while another dark, silent police officer, who must have been some kind of sergeant, sat by.

'Is your name Kevin Tregennis?'

'I go by every name and no name.'

'Yes. At the moment, I understand that you go under the name of Kelvin Trelawny.'

'My name in law is anything I want it to be.'

'And you have a false passport in that name.'

'How can it be false if that is my name?'

'Because it's Australian. And we know from the British authorities that it was forged.'

'I am a citizen of the world.'

The detective threw up is eyes and said,

'We can hold you for that for a while until…'

'Until what…?'

'Until we extradite you to Britain.'

'For what?'

'I think you know.'

'Where is my spy detector?'

'Spy detector? It's just a load of cardboard and Sellotape.'

The detective stared at him for a moment, trying to work out if he was being made fun of. Then he gave that famously Gallic shrug and got up to go.

Kevin spent the night in a police cell, which was cleaner and more comfortable than his digs.

CHAPTER SEVENTEEN

Danvers was not normally interested in the arts. At least, not as the arts were defined by arts programmes. However, he was very interested in the *Late Night Forum* report on Kelvin Trelawny. Like all such programmes, *Late Night Forum* was on when most people were asleep. They were watching in bed at Danvers' place.

'Do we have to watch this?' asked Fiona, as the woman who had just been appointed head of the Royal Shakespeare Company was explaining that talent was essentially a fascist concept and that what was needed in modern drama was more diversity. Her latest offering called SHOUT! involved people from minorities shouting abuse at the audience.

'It's very now,' she explained. Judging by the excerpts, it was indeed very now.

'I just want to see the next report,' said Danvers. Of course, Fiona knew very well it was going to be about Kevin. It was. They watched, he with fascination, she with one eyebrow permanently raised.

And now a report from Gavin Peach, our European correspondent about an English performance artist who has followed tradition by making Paris his spiritual home.

The news item showed a group of students, artists and critics demonstrating.

'They're very artistic, the French, aren't they?' said Fiona.

'Well, if by that, you mean that they took Jean Luc Goddard seriously, then yes, I suppose so.'

This protest – which includes the film director Martine Cresson - is against the intended extradition of performance artist Kelvin Trelawny on a charge of misappropriating dangerous military weapons.

A few of the demonstrators were interviewed. Some of them seemed to be under the impression that Kevin had stolen some nerve gas from NATO countries as a protest against chemical weapons. Another thought that artists should be able to do anything they wanted. Martine Cresson said that no-one should be in jail and everyone should be free. 'Oh dear,' said Danvers. 'This isn't what we intended at all. We must do something about this.'

'Like what?'

'I'm not sure. I was rather hoping for a less visible neutralisation of your husband. This won't do at all. We must think again.'

'Do you think they'll succeed?'

'It's possible. But I can't be sure. The French don't like extradition. They never extradite their own citizens. And you know what they're like with artists. They think anyone who owns a paintbrush is Paul Gauguin. And if it's a stolen paintbrush – so much the better.'

After another pause, he said, 'He really is something of a national nuisance, Mr Tregennis. I mean, an embarrassment to us all.'

A few days later, the French government announced that, owing to a pressure campaign from what it called 'significant artists', it would not be extraditing Mr Tregennis back to Great Britain. However, it made it quite clear that this was a temporary decision and would be reviewed at a later date, (i.e., when the fuss had died down). Mr Tregennis would be released on bail on the understanding that he would remain in Paris. Rumana called him to congratulate him,

'Why don't you come back anyway? It would look really good for you.'

'I will eventually. But I've just avoided extradition. It would look silly if I then went home.'

'No, it wouldn't. It would make you look innocent.'

'No. I need to get away from here. And in any case, because of the Schengen Agreement, technically if I go somewhere else, I haven't absconded. I'm still in Europe.'

Rumana thought this was a bit of a shaky argument from a legal point of view. But she said,

'No you can't. You've given your word. If you run away now, you'll look twice as guilty.'

'No, I need time. I need to put my case together. I need some help to get this thing out into the open. You can help me.'

'Oh, good grief, Kevin. You ask too much of me.'

'No, I don't. I've got a plan that will make your career.'

'My career is fine! Don't start making plans for me. I know what happens to your plans. They cause total devastation within a ten-mile radius.'

'I know what I'm doing, Rumana.'

She was too polite to laugh.

CHAPTER EIGHTEEN

Kevin managed to get a bus which took him most of the way until he could join the autoroute that would take him south. The *Autoroute du Soleil*, as it was known. Hitch-hiking now was not the danger it had been because the manhunt for him was over. At least until they found out he had disappeared.

After waiting an awful long time in a place where, he suspected, he was not supposed to be waiting, he finally managed to flag down an old Dutch couple in a camper van.

'Hello,' said the man, who was driving. 'Are you going far?'

'Probably farther than you are,' said Kevin.

The woman laughed and said, 'Give us a clue'. Being Dutch, they both spoke better English than Princess Anne.

'I'm heading for Spain,' said Kevin, which was not strictly true. He was on his way to the Algarve in Portugal, but the fewer people who knew that, the better.

'Hop in,' said the man. They both seemed very friendly.

Kevin climbed into the spacious van. He could smell the sickly odour of marijuana, an aroma which had always nauseated him. But the van was warm and cosy. He introduced himself. He told them his name was Geoffrey Amis. They were Hank and Gertha.

'We're going to Santiago de Compostela,' said the woman brightly.

Kevin knew this to be a favourite destination of Catholic pilgrims. They didn't look like pilgrims. More like heretics.

'Are you missionaries?' he asked, and they both laughed. No, they were not missionaries. They had friends there and were on a holiday. Kevin could see that most of their life had been a holiday. They were in their late sixties and had obviously grown up with the hippie movement – or some later variant of it. Hank was balding on top but had the obligatory ponytail. Gertha, like her husband, had once been good-looking, but too much sun, ill-advised recreational substances and a diet of brown rice had played merry hell with their complexions. They offered him a cigarette, which he checked to make sure it only contained tobacco.

They drove off. Gertha offered him lemonade and a wholemeal snack which tasted like polystyrene pellets. He thanked them but, no, really, he only wanted just the one. After a while, Gertha started to roll - with admirable dexterity given the fact that she was in a moving vehicle - a joint the size of a German sausage. The music system was playing something like Quintessence or the Mahavishnu Orchestra. Forty minutes of bum notes from spiritual nutters. But who was he to complain? They seemed like nice people, and they would take him a long way to his destination - probably without notifying the authorities. He started to relax. When would he learn?

They drove through the day and into the night. He must have dozed off here and there but they didn't seem to mind. Gertha offered him a blow-up pillow. Soon they were over the Spanish border and turning West for Bilbao. Eventually, it was too late to drive anymore, and they decided to stop in a deserted spot for the night. After all, this was a camper van. Kevin really had landed on his feet. Gertha broke out some food but despite his long journey, Kevin could not find the politeness to share their meal, whatever it was. After they had eaten and cleared up, the couple started preparing the sleeping arrangements. Kevin watched her and began to be a little suspicious. However, thanks to the fact that their English was so perfect, there was no room for misunderstandings. What impressed him was their grammatical perfection combined with a good grasp of colloquialisms. So, while he thanked them for their hospitality, he explained that he was by no means 'up for a threesome'. He took his bags and wandered off into the night. They didn't seem to take it personally and waved him off into the distance. Kevin hoped that he would not encounter any loose, rabid dogs for which the Iberian Peninsula was justly celebrated.

He walked on into the night. It was warm but he felt a chill, which possibly had more to do with his feeling of isolation and exile than the climate.

It was too late to hitch-hike. However, he realised that there was one factor operating in his favour. If this was a well-worn route for religious pilgrims, then it would be full of people making their way to the Cathedral at Santiago. Santiago was on the western tip of Spain which overhangs Portugal. Some of these pilgrims would be walking and some on bikes. But that was all to the good. He could blend into the landscape. Many people would be resting by the wayside if they couldn't make it to the 'comfort stations' which lined the route. Moreover, a lot of them would have walked over the high ground of France and would be exhausted. It wouldn't be in the least bit strange to see travellers asleep at the side of the road.

And so he lay down on his back in the dry grass. Above him, with arrestingly sharp delineation, was the miraculous crystal lattice of the zodiac. He wondered if he might be able to use it to navigate his way south. (The Galaxy's guide to the hitch-hiker.) He stared upwards for many minutes in awe-struck admiration for God's handiwork. Against the majesty of the cosmos, he felt a strange awareness of his own smallness. His eyes lost in the eternal glistening void, he suddenly felt no longer alone. Insignificant, but safe and at peace. The feeling was inexplicable, but it helped him sleep. That, and the fact that he was knackered.

And so he slept. And surprisingly, he did not sleep badly. When he awoke it was a beautiful day in lovely coastal countryside. He ate some corned beef and dry corn-flakes from his bag and then began to hitch-hike again. Once at Santiago, he could turn south and go all the way to the Algarve. It was by no means the shortest route, but he could stick to the coastal road and would not get lost. It was the most sensible plan for someone whose sense of direction could get himself lost in a lift.

He started hitch-hiking. Many of the drivers who went past him found something of ineluctable interest on the opposite side of the road. Kevin didn't blame them. Hitching was not as safe as it once had been. The world had changed. Sitting in your own home minding your own business was not as safe as it had been. Nonetheless, he would have liked to try it.

He wondered what Rumana was doing. Not standing on a roadside in the middle of nowhere like a bloody lemon, that was for sure. He hoped she was happier than he was. It was a cinch that she was, but you could never tell with someone so phlegmatic. Why did some people have such uncomplicated, such enviably uneventful lives?

Eventually a car stopped. It was an old banger of some kind. An Austin maybe. He wasn't sure. It was a two-toned car, red and rust. The red came from the original coat of paint and the rust colour came from the rust, which was the dominant artistic attitude. Kevin fancied that he could see steam coming out from under the car's bonnet.

'Quick,' said a voice with a Spanish accent. 'Get in.' Once again, it seemed to be obvious that Kevin was English. The driver looked like a drawing of a criminal from a nineteenth century textbook about genetic degradation among the lower orders. Only his forehead was hairless. But, thought Kevin, you shouldn't judge by appearances, so they say.

He jumped in and the car sped off, which is to say it started to move slightly faster than when it was stationary. The car was clearly used to taking its own time, but the driver himself was in a hurry. There was a sense of nervous anticipation about him. Clearly, he was some kind of devout pilgrim who, consumed with guilt, was keen to purge his sins on the steps of the great church as soon as possible. Kevin admired his religious passion. The man kept looking in the rear-view mirror with considerable agitation.

'Is everything OK?' asked Kevin.

'I just stole this car. You don't mind, huh?'

'No,' said Kevin, tiredly, leaning back resignedly in his seat. 'I don't mind.'

Suddenly, Santiago de Compostela, never mind the Algarve, seemed much further off. (Especially when the wheel came off and he was

148

back to hitch-hiking again.) Worse, once in Santiago, he was deprived of the flow of pilgrims. It took five more lifts and a great deal of time, to get to the south of Portugal. Kevin, however, was greatly encouraged by the fact that three of the five drivers were not lunatics.

CHAPTER NINETEEN

For a town without any character, Vale do Lobo, in the Algarve of Portugal, is a lovely place. It is full of large, detached houses called 'villas'. Some of these houses are owned by Brits and others by Germans. Many have swimming pools, since the sea is the Atlantic, not the Mediterranean, and the currents can be fierce. There are beach bars and cafes. In the mornings, the beach areas are quiet because the morning doesn't start until about 10.00am and you can't buy a breakfast until then. And when you do it is the usual continental inadequacy of coffee and croissants – symbolic of all that is wrong with Europe: too little, too late and too expensive. In the afternoons the bars play music loud enough to shake your bones to calcium powder.

Despite the risk of cost-free hitch-hiking, Kevin was still running short of money and he needed a job. He made his way to Zeno's Restaurant, about a mile back from the sea front.

The owner was Ronald Chard and Kevin knew him from way back, when he had been a wealthy trader in the City. Ronnie was a wiry, hirsute little eccentric with a cheery manner. He gave the impression of having military training but never spoke of it. Although not Scottish, he always celebrated Burns Night by standing on a table drunk, dressed only in his underwear and playing the bagpipes. Since retiring, he had developed a passion for buying expensive cars and doing them up. As the cars were generally in perfect condition when purchased, and as he was a largely useless mechanic, they tended to end up in worse nick than when he had bought them. He often sold them for a loss. But he could afford it. And his other hobby was golf which was no less of a daft

150

waste of time, energy and money. Kevin found Ronnie as he was just opening the restaurant.

'Kevin! What the hell are you doing here?' said his friend, who clearly did not study the news.

'Hello Ronnie. I'm afraid I'm in a bit of a mess. I need a job.'

This was brutal and possibly counterproductive honesty, since wealthy men like Ronnie often have a tendency to develop a distant look in their eyes when people start mentioning things like failure and impecuniousness. But he had at least asked for a job, not a loan. Kevin had, however, misjudged his man.

'Well, of course, my old chum. What can you do?'

'Anything. Literally anything. I'll clean the pond, do bar work and stock the shelves.'

There was a pause as Ronnie asked himself if he should enquire about the history of Kevin's misfortunes. But he decided against it.

'Well, I'll certainly find something for you. But most of the casual labour round here is done by Russian immigrants. They're cheaper than the Brits. Interestingly, they have the same reputation for drunken hooliganism.'

'Yes, I've heard. I wonder if it's anything to do with being a fallen empire?'

'Maybe so. Perhaps in a few years we'll be talking about the Americans in the same way.'

And so Kevin became an odd-job man. It was the most enjoyable job he had ever done. Ronnie gave him some cheap accommodation in a small but cosy flat over his garage. It was very quiet when Ronnie wasn't revving up cars underneath. Most of the time he wasn't because he was too busy with the restaurant and golfing. Kevin spent his days stocking shelves, cleaning the koi pond, cleaning the pool, serving customers and other bits and pieces. It was a beautiful place to work and the duties were light and varied. As long as Ronnie didn't find out about the Theory of the Division of Labour, he was in clover.

The restaurant itself was magnificent. It had a huge garden with a pool surrounded by Doric columns, designed by one of those people who didn't know that the original purpose of classical columns was to hold something up. Any ancient Greek who dined there might have asked what happened to the roof or perhaps would have suspected that hurricanes were prevalent in the area. But such people rarely showed up.

Customers were welcome to eat outside, as long as they didn't mind sharing their salads with flies the size and rapacity of herring gulls. There was a dark Portuguese girl called Maria who acted as a receptionist and waitress, a job she carried out with an unsettling lack of emotional disruption. If there was such a thing as a Latin temperament, nobody had told her.

And so Kevin was able to relax for a while. His flat was perfect: bijou, but functional. There was a bed, a table/desk and a little cooking top plus a kettle. It wasn't much, but his new situation gave him exactly what he wanted, which was space and time to think. He resolved to take advantage of this unexpected lull and do just that. He was fed up with flying by the seat of his pants all the time. He needed a plan. He looked for a piece of paper and a pen. That took up about ten minutes which gave him the curious delusion that he was doing something productive. He sat down at the table and wrote PLAN FOR ACTION at the top of the page. Things were really rolling now. He felt he was about to take control of events. Then he thought for about another ten minutes. He gazed out of the window. It was starting to get dark.

He wrote underneath the heading, RUMANA. He wondered what he could do about Rumana. He would come back to her.

MONEY. What to do about money? He thought for a minute. No ideas came. But at least he was confronting the problems, getting them in the front of his mind so he could evaluate and resolve them.

MONEY. How could he earn a living? He had a job but that hardly paid enough to get him out of trouble. He needed a proper source of income. He wrote next to it, credit cards. £5000. That was good. He put a double tick next to that. That was a real positive. That meant he could put one tick next to Rumana. He was really getting somewhere now. He gazed out of the window again for a few moments. Then he crossed RUMANA out.

Then he realised that he might not be able to use his credit cards. They might have been frozen, like his bank account. Or they might be used to trace him. One of them was back in England and the other one was halfway up to the limit. He cursed himself for not using it to draw out cash. It would have destroyed his credit rating because he had no means of paying it back, but that was a distant problem. Anyway, he had broken the back of the planning schedule.

He wanted a cigarette, so he went outside and had one. Then he came back inside, made a cup of coffee and came back to the table. It was dark now. He switched on the table lamp. He needed to get a move on. He wrote RUMANA again. Then he put 1) Propose to her 2) Take it slowly 3) Go and see her parents. He thought about that last one for a while. They were Muslims. They weren't very devout but it was a problem. Better get Rumana onside first. He crossed out 3).

The piece of paper was filling up nicely. Ideas were flowing. He was brainstorming. Sooner or later, he would hit the jackpot. He was surprised he hadn't thought of this method before.

Then, in a moment of inspiration, he started thinking laterally, outside the box. He wrote, HOBBY – Take up painting. Then he ticked it. It was now very dark outside. Next to that he wrote – Does Rumana like painting? We could go to the National Gallery.

He stared hard at the piece of paper. Then he suddenly screwed it up and threw it in the bin. He went to bed. In the morning, he went to his job and hoped for inspiration.

One night, Chard invited him over to have dinner with him. Maria cooked it and served silently, drifting wispily in and out like a family ghost. It was a restful evening and Kevin experienced the bittersweet feeling of being pulled into a warm and friendly family orbit, knowing that at some time – probably quite soon - he would be wrenched out of it again.

The meal began quietly enough as Chard was a man of few words when sober, while Maria was a woman of few words in all circumstances.

Kevin wondered why. Perhaps she had some inner anguish which she suppressed. Maybe she fought hard every day to quell the agonised sobs of a broken heart. Perhaps she had only just been told about the death of Rudolph Valentino. Another possibility was that she was just a rude and miserable cow. The truth would probably never be known, since she would never speak of it.

As for Kevin, he was lost in his own problems. Gradually, however, Chard, the Scotsman manque, began to respond to the whiskey and loosen up.

'I was in the forces you know.'

'Yes, you have that air,' said Kevin softly.

'Saw a lot of action. Iraq and so forth. They used to call me Mad Mick. My name isn't Mick, but Mad Mick is more alliterative. Army nicknames are like that.'

'Yes, that makes sense.'

'I killed a man once.'

'Difficult to avoid in your profession, I should think.'

These quiet exchanges were separated by little pauses.

'I wasn't in the forces at the time. Nobody ever found out. It was an argument over a woman.'

Kevin wondered why Chard was telling him this now. Chard liked a drink and often went a bit wild under its influence. But he was one of those men who could handle his liquor and control it. Kevin sensed that he had never told anyone this story before.

Maria drifted in and out as if on a cushion of air. But her presence did not stop Chard from talking. She didn't give the impression of being a careless gossip.

'I was in the intelligence services, you know.'

'I didn't know that, no.'

'I'm more ashamed of that than I am of having killed someone in anger.'

He poured himself another whiskey with deliberate competence.

'It's a mad world. Cutthroat trading in the City was a breath of fresh air by comparison.'

'Yes, I can imagine.'

'They're accountable to no-one, you know. The intelligence services, I mean.'

Kevin nodded.

'They live in a world of their own. A Wild West where people are excused moral considerations. And all justified by the suggestion that the others behave the same way.'

Kevin nodded again and Chard was silent for a few moments. But Kevin knew he was not finished yet. He was working his way up to something. He took another swig and then said,

'Do you know what a false flag operation is?'

'Yes, of course. It's where one intelligence agency commits some outrage in order to bring another one into disrepute.'

Chard nodded.

'I bet you thought they only existed in thrillers?'

Kevin thought no such thing, so he shrugged. Naturally he could fill in the rest. Chard had been a party to some such enormity while he had been an intelligence operative.

The man was silent again as though he were mentally masticating his subject, chewing it into digestible form.

'Don't tell me,' said Kevin finally. 'I don't need to know. And truthfully, I have enough dangerous information at the moment.'

'Yes. That I figured,' said Chard slowly.

Kevin tried to work out what Chard was trying to do. Warn his guest about intelligence and spying? Hardly any need for that now. Or soften him up with a shameful secret so that Kevin would be more relaxed about telling his? Perhaps it was a well-known intelligence trick. Kevin realised with utter horror that despite all his failures in life, he would have made a good spy. But whatever Chard had wanted, he said no more. As if snapping out of a trance, he shouted in a bad Scots accent, 'We'll ha'e the pipes now, will we not?'

For once Maria's stony face betrayed exactly what she thought of this prospect as she fetched the bagpipes for him. It took her a while. She may have thrown them out, hoping he wouldn't notice and now had to fetch them from a skip. Naturally, Chard stood on the table to play *Bonnie Black Isle*. But in deference to Maria's presence, he kept his trousers on.

Afterwards, Chard and Kevin had a game of chess. Chard beat him in only a few moves. They played again with the same result. Then Maria played Kevin and she also beat him.

'Sometimes she beats me as well,' said Chard laughing, something he did very rarely.

Then they had cheese and biscuits plus some appropriate liquor for Chard. Eventually it was time for Kevin to go back to his little flat. Chard offered to walk him down the drive from the house.

'You're a writer, aren't you?' he asked Kevin.

'Well, I'm a journalist. There's an ongoing dispute about whether that's the same thing.'

'I've been writing a book.'

'Really? Well, that's exciting. How far have you got?'

'First three chapters.'

'Aah. That's often where the trouble sets in. How long have you been at it?'

'Twenty years.'

'Bloody hell. What's the problem?'

Chard thought for a while and said,

'I think I've said everything I have to say.'

'But you're...I mean a man with your background...the things you've seen and done?'

'I didn't say I'd said everything I *could* say. I've just said everything I *have* to say.'

'Oh dear. You'd never make a journalist, that's for sure. Our job is to fill space with words. We're actively encouraged to do that. The only resistance we get is from the advertising people.'

As they reached the garage complex, Chard said goodnight. Again, it was as though he wanted to say more to Kevin but had decided not to.

He was a man of few words. It wasn't until Kevin was alone and going to bed that he realised that Chard knew all about his troubles and what was causing them. He had wanted him to know that they were not over and that he could expect more trouble, but without revealing how much he knew. Perhaps Chard couldn't decide whether he wanted Kevin to go or stay. Loyalty to a friend versus self-preservation. But he kept everything to himself. Old habits die hard with spies.

One morning, after he had been there a week or so, Kevin was stacking the bottles behind the bar when one of the agency cleaning ladies came in. She was about forty-five and a brunette. She was a little more Junoesque than Kevin normally found attractive - but who was he to complain considering the shape he was in?

'Hello. I'm Kevin. I haven't seen you before.'
'Oh, hello. I am Luba. I had to go back to the Ukraine. I am Russian but I have children there. My husband is dead and my mother looks after them.'
'Oh, I'm sorry about your husband. Are the children in danger?'
'So far, no. They live in the west of the country. But things are difficult.'
'I can imagine.'
She had a nice, shy and apologetic smile which he liked. It was what he had found so compelling about Rumana. And she seemed to like him, without which all other considerations are irrelevant. They chatted for a while until Luba decided that she had better get on with her chores. He offered to take her for a pizza later on and she agreed.

The pizza place was a long way from the affluent part of the region where the villas grew, and he had no car. But Luba did and offered to collect him. This was just as well since Kevin had little experience of driving on the left, except when he shouldn't have done. She wore a red striped sundress; he had managed to resist the temptation to wear shorts, even though it was blazing hot. Her English was terrible but they both spoke fluent French.

They had a lot in common. Her husband had been unfaithful while he was alive. They had both begun their lives with much promise, but bad decisions had caused the sunlit uplands of the affluent society to darken for them. Kevin was vague about his previous troubles, saying simply, 'Yes, I've been there.' And indeed, he *had* been there. What he didn't tell her was that he lived there with permanent residency status.

He liked Luba, although she was by no means a light-hearted person. She had that curious Russian sadness of the soul. It really does exist and he could see it when she drifted off into a sad reverie, when she seemed to be staring off into the vastness of the Eurasian plains.

The meal was a success and she agreed to see him again. However, she did not want to come back to his flat as she wanted to take things slowly if that was all right with him. He concurred and she suggested a long walk along the cliffs toward the beach on their next mutual day off. He said yes and they agreed to start very early as she had some chores to do later in the morning.

He felt good when he returned to his little flat, but life was swift to take back the stolen moments of elation. Rumana called. This caused his spirits to fall, firstly because he realised that he still loved her. And secondly because she told him some terrible news.

'Kevin, I'm so sorry. Your mother is dead.'

He was unable to say anything for a few moments. Then he slowly thanked her and said he would call her back when he was feeling better. He was very grateful to her, especially for looking in on his mother. He owed her so much and wanted to give her everything. The only problem was, he had nothing, and she didn't want what he had.

He sat down on his bed and thought of his relationship with his mother, another failure. She had been eighty-seven. Kevin wondered what it must be like to be eighty-seven. You see your entire life, knowing all of it exactly, except that it was behind you instead of ahead of you, time and choice rendered meaningless. The whole story is known and if you could be nearly ninety but imagine that you were twenty, then you would be seeing it as though gifted with some kind of bizarre retrospective prescience. Your entire existence set out before and behind you, immutable and inevitable. Every dream shattered, every effort wasted and every hope that returns to mock you. And nothing to be done about any of it. Like one of those Bollywood farces, where the action is constructed around whatever sets and props are available at the time. An obstacle course that laughs at the idea of free will.

He slept badly, but found the next day that his work helped him to cope. He hated himself for admitting that he would be able to get over his mother quite easily.

When he met Luba on Thursday, he told her of his loss. She was very sorry. She understood the pain of loss. She told him of her family history

– half Ukrainian and half Russian - and the appalling tribulations they had suffered (as much from Stalin as from Hitler). After that, they fell silent. They walked for a while without speaking. However, he did not want to lose this opportunity with her, so he began to chatter, idly about his mother, and how he had wanted to know her better but had never seemed to have the time, always putting off his visits. He was aware that he may have been saying too much.

As they walked toward the beach along the hill crest, near to the golf courses, she fell behind him and he hardly noticed as he rambled on in self-pity. They were completely alone. There was nobody out on the course next to them; it was too early. It was only by chance that he turned and saw that she was pulling a gun out of her bag. She was obviously a trained professional assassin and there was no point in reasoning with her, so he simply hit her with all the force at his disposal. His punch connected better than his kisses, and he managed to knock her over. This gave him time to start running - but she wasn't stunned. She was soon up and drawing a bead on him. Kevin tore like mad down the cliff bank where the trees might give him some cover. It was a plan, but only a temporary expedient. At the moment, any action he took might turn out to be temporary. He heard a shot but he kept running on the assumption that he was not yet dead. Then he heard another shot. There was a road down at the bottom of the steep bank and he cascaded down towards it. One of his deck shoes flew off and he trod on something that might have been a clump of nettles and lego bricks. He shouted in pain but kept going, running and limping like a lunatic on an army assault course, travelling in a crazy-paving diagonal downwards – a path which seemed metaphorically familiar to him - jumping between trees and zig-zagging to avoid incoming bullets.

Luba - if that was really her name - had been standing on the top of the crest but now she started to follow him down. She moved more cautiously than Kevin. She probably knew that he was not in any shape to run for much longer. His chest felt as if it were about to explode. He wished he had a gun but even then, she would have had the advantage of superior skill and marksmanship. He reached a large tree and stopped. He was half dead, which meant that she only had to supply the other half to win her monthly assassin's bonus. Almost vomiting with terror and exhaustion, he hid behind the tree. She stopped halfway down and fired two more shots. They both hit the tree. Huge chunks of bark and sap flew off. He wasn't an expert on firearms but she must have had some kind of Magnum. The bullets exploded like mortar bombs. He looked down. He was nearly at the road which ran along the bottom of the hill. Across the road was another golf course – they were plentiful in Vale Do Lobo. It was probably Portuguese for 'valley of golf courses'. On this one, a few golfers had started to appear.

Kevin had to make a snap decision. Either stay here where there was some cover which would protect him for a while, but not for long – or run out into the open in the hope that she would not kill him while there were witnesses about. But perhaps she didn't care about witnesses. No doubt her controllers wanted him dead at all costs, regardless of the fallout. No doubt once the job was successfully completed, they would whisk her out of the country and back to Russia, where she would be decorated as a national heroine and gifted with a lifetime supply of turnips.

Another shot made up his mind and he ran downwards in the direction of the golfers. He could see now that one of them was Ronnie Chard who was just teeing off with an almighty swing. He was an amazing golfer. He should have been, the practice he put in. Luba stopped again to take another shot. She didn't fire wildly. She wanted to hit Kevin in the head, where it would cause him the most inconvenience. Suddenly, she looked up. She may, just for a nanosecond, have seen the golf ball before it brained her.

Kevin collapsed on the road, panting like a decrepit racing whippet. Chard ambled towards him, trundling his little golf trolley. Kevin could see Chard's golfing partner standing at the tee, hands on hips, looking bewildered. Ignoring Kevin, who was trying to remember how to breathe again, Ronnie left the cart at the side of the road and walked across to where Luba was lying. He poked at her a few times with his Titleist TSR2 Fairway Wood. (Some pros recommend a driver for this job.) Then he checked her neck pulse. Kevin could see that he had touched corpses many times before.

'Dead,' he said after a few seconds. 'Teach her to fire guns while I'm teeing off.'

He turned back to Kevin.

'It's a very strict convention, you know. No coughs, sudden movements or assassination attempts while a player is concentrating. Having a spot of bother, old chum?'

He picked up his golf ball and held it up so that his partner could see it.

'Found it!' he said. The man in the distance gave him the thumbs up. After a while, Kevin felt that he could talk again.

'Did you actually do that deliberately?'

'That would be telling. Now, I think you have a few explanations for me.'

'I will never, ever call golf a stupid game again.'

'I didn't know that you had. It's a good job I didn't know that when I teed off. I might have hit you instead.'

They all went back to Chard's car and thence to his salubrious villa where Maria – Kevin only now realised that she lived in with Chard – who had once been a nurse, silently fixed Kevin's foot. And if she cared very deeply about his pain and anguish, her emotional restraint was admirable.

Kevin explained his situation to Chard, who simply said,

'Sorry, old fruit, but I will have to call the police. I have my situation here to think about.'

Kevin said he understood.

There was nowhere to run or hide now. If the Russians could find him then anyone could obviously track him down with ease. He must come into the open now as it was the only safe place. He must face whatever the world could throw at him. And now that someone had tried to kill him, his story looked better. He looked like a victim - which was his proper station in life. The police arrived quickly and he told them his story.

They say that the police always know if a prisoner is guilty or not. The innocent cannot sleep and pace about in their cells in worry or terror. The guilty, realising that the flight and fight are over, are suffused with relief and sleep like the innocent are supposed to sleep. Kevin was in the same position. It was all over, and he felt a completely irrational sense of well-being. He was caught. Now they would extradite him.

CHAPTER TWENTY

The Portuguese authorities held Kevin for a few days. They offered him a lawyer but he refused. He did not wish to challenge extradition. Eventually, they sent him back to Britain.

The British police arrested Kevin at Heathrow Airport. There was a lot of reporters there. He would be the only one who didn't get the story. The story of his life.

Kevin was taken to the police station and was charged with stealing government property. They didn't specify which government it was. After they had processed and charged him, they locked him in a cell before his preliminary hearing. They let Rumana come to see him.

He didn't know what to say to her, so he said, 'Thanks for everything you've done.'

'Obviously it wasn't enough. Is there anything else I can do?'

'Yes, if I get out of this, you can marry me.'

'I'm already married,' she said, lifting up her ring finger. He was stunned for a moment, even though he had known she was engaged. It cost him everything he had to say, 'Congratulations'.

A defence lawyer was appointed. His name was Smethwick: a dull-looking, bespectacled pen-pushing, disinterested, blasé timeserver. Kevin didn't like him. He could see that he didn't believe Kevin was not guilty and looked as though he was marching in time until he got his pension.

'Defend yourself?' said Smethwick. 'That's never a good idea.'

'I know. That's probably why I thought of it. I'm a fountain of bad ideas. Do you remember The Black Death? That was my idea.'

'Er...yes. The problem is this: you don't know anything about...erm...things like precedent and courtroom procedure.'

'Good. That'll make it easier to write the novel.'

Smethwick took a deep breath and then persisted. He didn't care but it was what he was paid to do.

'You know nothing about the law.'

'I know a lot about what happened.'

'Good. Tell me what happened and then I'll know as well.'

Kevin could see he wouldn't believe him but he told him anyway. After he had finished, the lawyer started speaking. Kevin didn't listen. He even suspected that Smethwick was there to make sure he didn't get off. Or was he just developing a persecution complex?

The lawyer rambled on and on, but Kevin had given up. Rumana being married was the last blow. He would defend himself. He was all he had.

CHAPTER TWENTY-ONE

The prosecution opposed bail at the preliminary hearing, but Kevin was able to convince the judge that he had come home voluntarily after calling the police. He could have run off, he explained. This was a matter of record, even if they didn't believe his story about an assassination attempt. The prosecutor argued that he had only come home when it was unavoidable. But the judge was lenient. Kevin made his way home.

It was strange the way he could feel Fiona's absence when he returned to the house. He knew as soon as he walked in that she had gone. There was a note on the table saying that she had met someone else and that she had left him. (P.S. Shave that stupid beard off.) There was also an Ansafone message telling him about the note. She had sent him a text message telling him about the Ansafone message.

He was greeted by a conflicting mix of aromas, redolent of neglect and abandonment. Most unsettling of all was the rancid smell of the two dead goldfish in the bowl on the back windowsill. They were floating like two miniature naval war victims. Kevin was shocked. They had been her fish. How mercurial were her affections. It was a good job they hadn't had any children.

She seemed to have been very exact in what she had taken. All her clothes, all her books and a few household utensils. He searched the kitchen drawers just knowing that she would have taken the tin opener. She had. The few tins in the pantry were useless. And even the goldfish were too far gone for an eater as undiscriminating as Kevin. There was no other food in the house, so he opted for a takeaway curry, a waste of his very limited resources. This choice was largely territorial since it meant that his own odour dominated the other unpleasant spoors of the recently vacated house.

Once he had eaten, he went upstairs to the study and switched on the computer. He typed up his entire story. It took him over two hours. Then he sent a copy to Rumana saying,

Dearest Rumana, This is my wedding gift to you. It should net you a Pulitzer Prize. Don't send it to a British newspaper otherwise they will D-notice it. I think they're called Public Interest Immunity certificates. Send it to the New York Times. Those bastards hate Britain almost as much as they hate Donald Trump and Israel. They'll use it for sure.

Then he went to bed. There is a certain feeling you get as late middle age approaches old age: it is that life is so short, but seems never to end.

CHAPTER TWENTY-TWO

The trial started in the usual mundane way. After the tip staff had finished warming up the audience by doing his swearing-in schtick, a barrister called Mrs Denison laid out the prosecution case which involved the Official Secrets Act, treason, malice aforethought with prejudice hereafter referred to and vouchsafed without demur, charged on indictment appertaining to the abstraction of military stuff, M'lud, if it please the court in the name of the King. Then she introduced her esteemed colleagues. It was announced that Mr Kevin Tregennis, the defendant would be defending himself. This caused the judge to throw his eyes up, and a ripple of rhubarbs went through the members of the public. The judge called for some semblance of order by banging his Sisson and Parker fountain pen (excellent value at £1 - 9 shillings and sixpence – you'll never need another!) on his desk. The jury was told by the judge not to be influenced by the newspapers, which advice seemed to astonish some of them.

And off they went. Kevin's life was about to be examined and decided by lawyers, journalists and spies, the unholy trinity from the pit.

The charge was led by the experienced Mrs Denison, whose wig balanced precariously on top of a steel wool perm. She began by telling the jury and the judge that she would prove beyond a shadow of a doubt that the accused was never a member of or working for or in any way associated with the British Secret Intelligence Service. She then called her first witness in: MI6 case officer X. Case officer X would be hidden behind a special screen to guard his identity. The court watched in amazement as he walked in wearing a false beard and dark glasses.

They found it most amusing. He went immediately behind the screen. Kevin knew who it was, especially when he began to speak. It was Danvers. This curious spectacle reminded him of the Matrix Churchill Affair where the SIS had protected themselves by selling their own agents down the river.

The prosecution began with the ridiculous sight of Mrs Denison seemingly interrogating a blank screen.

'Mr X, you are an employee of the Secret Intelligence Services better known as MI6, are you not?'

'I am.'

'And this is the international service, as opposed to MI5 which deals with counterintelligence domestically?'

'That is correct.'

'Is it in any way possible that the accused could have been working for MI6 over the past year?'

'Not at all. Such a large and complex and indeed dangerous operation would have had to be approved at the very highest of levels.'

'Which dangerous and complex operation is this?' asked the judge.

'The theft of a sample of lethal nerve gas by a British agent, M'Lud,' said Mrs Denison. The judge nodded and said 'oh' as though he had just realised this was yet another of those tedious stolen nerve gas cases. Mrs Denison continued.

'I see, thank you. Almost the entire organisation would have to know about it?'

'Well, no, I like to think that we only share information about operations with those who need to know. But there would most certainly be evidence of involvement which could be referred to. These things aren't done on the hoof.'

Kevin stood up.

'I'm sorry to interrupt, M'lud, but the very point I am making is that this did not begin as a highly complex and planned major operation. The mission which the witness asked me to carry out began as a routine drop and collect mission. At least those were his words. But the nature of that operation was altered by unforeseen circumstances.'

'You will have a chance to put your case in due course, Mr Tregennis,' said the judge.

The prosecution began again.

'Is it likely, Mr X, that such an encounter could have happened by accident?'

'Please don't ask the witness to speculate, Mrs Denison.'

'Thank you, M'lud,' said Kevin.

But the judge interrupted, as something was worrying him.

'One moment, please Mrs Denison. Are you saying, Mr Tregennis, that the witness is known to you?'

'Yes, M'lud. I recognise the voice. He gave his name to me as Danvers. It would be more helpful if I could identify him personally.'

'I'm afraid it wouldn't, M'lud,' said Mrs Denison, 'since it would simply be a question of the witness's word against the accused. Besides, it would be against the public interest if Mr X's identity were revealed and his security status compromised.'

'I see,' said the judge.

'However, the matter is easily solved, M'lud,' said Mrs Denison. 'Case Officer X, is your name Danvers?'

'It is not,' replied Danvers. 'And I have never seen the accused before in my life.'

'Then,' said Kevin, 'I can call another witness who can identify that he went to my house and spoke to my wife. This witness sent me a photo of them. I confirmed her description.'

'I'm afraid it isn't that easy, Mr Tregennis,' said the judge. 'This isn't television. You can't just pull witnesses out of thin air. They have to be assessed and identified prior to the court case.'

'But this is urgent, M'lud. I can prove he is perjuring himself.'

The prosecution objected energetically. Mrs Denison cited precedent. Why there was a case just like it during the witch hunts prior to the Civil War, if she could quote the well-known case of Silas Norbet versus the Crown in which...

'Yes, yes,' said the judge, looking at his watch. Perhaps he had a lunch. 'This is where you have a problem of defending yourself, Mr Tregennis. You cannot cite legal precedent,' he added.

'Yes I can, M'lud. I can cite the precedent of other cases where a surprise witness was called – and I bet you know what they are.'

There were many cheers from the audience. Kevin seemed to have some support somewhere. A few applauded and some whooped. The judge told them to be quiet, which they were for a time. Then they erupted again with whoops and cheers. Kevin wondered if they all worked at Chevron.

As for his request, the judge apologised, but there was nothing he could do. The case was one involving national security. Without a better reason, he was not able to risk exposing the cover of the case officer in the witness box. Rumana was not able to testify. Kevin felt very stupid that he hadn't requested that Rumana be a witness. But how could he have possibly known that they would have had the purblind and arrogant crease to send Danvers to the court? Rumana left in a hurry. Kevin was sure that she had done her best, but he was mortified that she would run out like that.

In fact, Rumana had hurried away to the offices of the Globe. She had had an idea. She managed to get through the security desk without an identity pass. They didn't know that she had resigned, and they still remembered her face. She told them she had forgotten her pass and they gave her a temporary one. For all they knew she had been on vacation for a few weeks. She got the lift up to the fourth floor and went to Amis' office. Amis was just coming out, either going to lunch, or going to an appointment or going for a drink somewhere, or going to see his PA to arrange a lunch or a drink with someone.

'Romania!' said Amis, who was clearly in a jolly mood. 'How are you? Back for a visit already? Had an attack of conscience and want to return all the stationery?'

'It's Rumana. Hello Geoff. I'm fine. Can I see you about something urgent?'

'Well, I am in a bit of a hurry...'

'It's really urgent.'

'Well, OK but I can only give you five minutes.'

He waved her into the little airlock that he called his office. He indicated a chair the other side of his desk and they both sat.

'If you want your old job back, I'm afraid no can do. I promoted the guy who cleans the windows.'

He laughed. Rumana smiled.

'As long as you didn't promote the guy who services the latte machine.'

'Yeeeesss! Well, Rumana, what can I do for you?'

Amis grinned what he thought was his captivating and charming grin. In fact, he looked like a man who was being forced to listen to his boss's daughter playing the banjo.

'It's complicated.'

'Yes, I'm sure it is, but as I say, I'm very busy you know.'

'Unless there's a good story in it.'

'Exactly.'

There was a pause.

'Well...is there a good story in it?'

'It's about this court case involving Kevin.'

Amis had already lost interest. He waved the idea away.

'You must be joking. We want to keep the paper out of that as much as possible. National security and all that. Anyway, what's happened to him is his own fault.'

'Oh no, really it isn't,' she said, leaning excitedly over the desk. 'He's being fitted up. The SIS asked him to spy for them and now they won't admit it.'

Amis leaned back and put his fingertips together. This was an easy one to deflect.

'Well, he should have come home when they told him to. Could have cleared himself. Instead, he runs off to Portugal in a false moustache like some cockney bank blagger. Silly bugger. Anyway, we can't comment on an ongoing court case. It's contempt or something. Our legal people would have double hernias.'

'Yes, but what if there was a big story and it wasn't contempt?'

Amis said nothing. He was being sold to. Never say anything when you're being sold to. And in any case, he wasn't that interested. Rumana persevered.

'It's about this man...'

She showed Amis the picture she had taken of Danvers. He took the phone from her and looked at it. It seemed to have a very strange effect on him. It may have been the flickering lighting from the suspended ceiling combined with the darkness of the office but she could have sworn that he was changing colour like some exotic jelly fish. First white, then red, then purple.

'Thompson,' he said through his teeth.

'His name is Danvers. He's an MI6 operative.'

'He told me he was called Thompson,' said Amis, as if that were the crime he hated him for. But he managed to take hold of himself.

'Anyway, we can't interfere, like I said.'

But Rumana could see he was interested.

'Oh, but you can because he claims that he *wasn't* involved in it. He's claiming that he isn't there. He can't object to having his photo in the paper without admitting that he is.'

Amis looked at her with sinister satisfaction. And then he looked again at the photo. Then he squinted, and the first effect which the photo had had on him was nothing compared with what happened now. He rose slowly from his seat.

'That's Fiona,' he said.

'Yes, that's right. Kevin's wife. They're having an affair.'

Amis swore deliberately and forcefully. Rumana didn't quite understand this reaction but she knew that she had made a convert somehow. Amis sank down again into his chair and went into a silent, multicoloured meltdown. He looked as though he was going to crush the phone in his hand.

Finally – it took a long time – he again managed to collect himself.

'Tell me what you want me to do.'

'Just stick it on the front of the paper. And then, if you can, put another next to it with a false beard added. Say something oblique about the court case and then ask if these are the same man.'

'I'll put this to Sandra in the legal department. If she says it's not actionable then we're in business. I think this can be done.'

He left her in the office for a few minutes while he arranged things with the legal and then the production people. When he returned, he asked her to send the picture to his phone so that he could pass it on. Then he sat down again. He was a changed man - ten years younger and with the fresh complexion of someone who expected only the good things from life. He stared once more at the photo and then said to her, 'Fancy a latte?'

'Actually, I'm quite hungry.'

'Yes, me too. Let's go somewhere and eat.'

And then, smiling in a kind of near ecstasy, he said,

'I fancy something served piping hot right down the front of the trousers.'

Rumana nodded and smiled back. She no longer expected anybody or anything to make sense.

They left to go to his favourite restaurant. Whatever Rumana had done, she had pushed the right buttons. She had succeeded but she didn't know how.

CHAPTER TWENTY-THREE

When the paper came out the next day, the whole country erupted. Or at least the media did, and they knew of no other world but their own. The front page of the Globe did not exactly explain what the connection of Danvers to the case was, except in a very elliptical way. They just printed a photo of him, suggested he was an MI6 operative, asked why he was committing adultery with the woman in the picture and then presented a photo kit picture of him with a beard and dark glasses.

The TV companies picked it up and ran with the scoop. The next day, the other papers joined in like a howling mob of football hooligans kicking a corpse. They didn't have to report on the court case itself, but they *could* report on the fact that the Globe had printed the story. As with other such stories, the whole thing spread like a pneumonic pestilence.

Questions were asked by the media and avoided by politicians. A Labour MP from one of the inner London constituencies demanded that Parliament be recalled. It was pointed out to her that Parliament did not have to be recalled as it was already in session. In fact, she had been speaking in parliament when she had made the demand.

The case of Crown against Tregennis collapsed. The court went wild with joy. Kevin was mobbed by the people and had to fight his way out. On the steps of the building, he was presented with a large, unfragrant bouquet of media microphones. A Belgian TV reporter asked him how he felt.

'Well, Brian, I feel great. I just trapped the ball, moved in front of the goal area and tapped it into the back of the net.'

180

'Pardon me?'

'What will you do now?' asked another.

'Well, I'm studying a lot of offers at the moment. The Aga Khan wants me to be his ambassador to West Bromwich Albion. I intend to make some choices as soon as my agent is released from Broadmoor. I have lots of plans. I've been putting off skateboarding up the Orinoco for a while now. Also, I intend to write someone else's autobiography – either Kylie Minogue or Joseph Stalin. I haven't decided. Thank you for your interest.'

He tried to push through the melee but the microphones closed in on him, like the metal teeth of some vicious classical monster.

'You will do something creative?' said someone with a French accent.

'No, my accountant has already tried that. He gets released next week as well. However, I do have my musical comedy about haemorrhoids to finish.'

'Will you take legal action?'

'Most definitely. I intend to make legal history by suing myself. Although I expect there to be a hefty out-of-court settlement. Excuse me, I think that's my bus.'

And with that, he pushed his way through the throng and made his way home.

Kevin saw a great deal of Rumana after that. He helped her write the book which won her the Pulitzer Prize for Journalism, which prize was open to foreign entrants. He wanted her to get all the credit and the money for it in gratitude for the help she had given him when he had had no-one else. If he still loved her, he never said anything about it.

Perhaps he had finally given up. She didn't think he looked well – he often seemed tired and distracted - but they managed to put the project together. He talked and she wrote. But he was often vague and she had to do a lot of authentication and research.

But when it was all finished, she never saw him again. In their last conversation, she told him she was pregnant and would be concentrating on her family in the future. She told him that Amis had called her and offered her a huge salary to come back to the paper but she had refused.

What happened to Danvers was never clear. He was unlikely to have prospered in his profession after the case but, as he was a man of private means, this did not matter too much. He did not marry Fiona, as she had become tired of him, and started having an affair with one of the neighbours on his estate up north.

CHAPTER TWENTY-FOUR

Stress, smoking, bad diet and a lack of sleep took their inevitable toll on Kevin. One night he awoke to find that he had been sleeping on his left arm. He could feel the pins and needles. But when he turned over onto his right side, the blood did not seem to flow back into his arm. It continued to tingle. He was perspiring heavily. On getting up to switch on the light he felt dizzy and when he went back to bed, he had difficulty breathing.

For some reason, he felt really stupid googling the symptoms. He was hoping it would say 'panic attack', but it didn't. He called an ambulance and was soon in hospital, although he could remember very little about the journey.

The doctors told him afterwards that they had almost lost him. They sternly told him to give up smoking and watch his diet and health. Kevin had hoped that Rumana would come to see him, but she didn't. Neither did Fiona. Neither did anybody. After being released from hospital, he became something of a recluse. But he knew that this could not last. At some time, he would need to re-join the world of honest labour.

He took the doctors' advice and only dined on their recommended diet, which tasted like moist tissue and kapok and which left him feeling ravenous. But he did successfully lose a bit of weight and could now fit comfortably into his old suit. He couldn't do the jacket buttons up, but he was in it and ready for action, if he didn't walk too fast. He felt a lot better and wondered if he could find some work. He was nowhere near retirement and needed an income. What could he do? All he knew was journalism and that is very close to knowing nothing.

However, Kevin knew that he had one important thing to do which he had been putting off for too long. He left the house and drove out to the country towards the care home where his mother had spent her last years. At the back of the home was a little cemetery garden. It was private and enclosed by a wall, although somehow that hadn't stopped the local teenagers from using it as a drinking den. He could see the bottles and cigarette ends lying around on the resting places of people's loved ones. He could smell urine.

His mother's burial had been organised by the home staff. They seemed to have done a nice job in accordance with her last wishes. No doubt Leonora would have been in attendance overseeing the arrangements. Thomas would have put in an appearance to see if there was any money for him in the will. In the corner of the little enclosure was an unpretentious gravestone with a line from the Bible.

Madeleine Tregennis

1935-2022

Beloved mother of Leonora, Thomas and Kevin

'Her children shall rise up and call her blessed.' - Proverbs 31:28.

The verse made Kevin feel very guilty. He stumbled over a makeshift prayer in his mind. But the prayer and the tears that flowed were, he knew, for himself. He stayed until he no longer felt uncomfortable leaving.

Once back at the house, he looked for useful things to do. He needed to get his life pointed in some purposeful direction.

He found his unfinished novel buried in the chaos of his computer screen in a file marked *Finish This Now Before You Do Anything!* It was called *Death Flies in Formation by Brett Tungsten, 2015.* He remembered being very pleased with the opening hook.

'Kruger's grip tightened on the handgun, as the two stormtroopers walked stealthily but unsuspectingly toward him. And to think, only a moment earlier, Gertrude had been breathing lustfully in his arms...'

Perhaps it needed a bit more work. Too much work to be an immediate money-spinner.

There was also his musical about Robin Hood and Maid Marion. With a cast of thousands, there were more parts than there were people alive in the Middle Ages (although the role of Friar Tuck could be doubled up by Woman with Pitchfork). He needed ideas. Perhaps his brother Tom could give him one. But he would need a collaborator for a musical as he had no ear for music. Perhaps that could wait too.

He tried to sell the house. It was on the market for weeks. He only had one interested party. A middle-aged couple came and looked over the property in silence. Eventually the woman said, 'How very original. Six junk rooms.'

On a whim he called up the Globe, having convinced himself that they owed him something, a point of view which Amis could not be guaranteed to share. But when he was put through to the editor, it was not Amis who answered the phone but Sarah Markstein.

'Kevin,' she purred like an electric hedge trimmer, 'my darling one.'

'Sarah? Are you the new editor?'

'Yes, is that all right with you, Kevin?'

'Oh yes, absolutely. Congratulations. What happened to Geoff?'

'Oh, Geoff has gone somewhere where he can make better use of his talents.'

'Oh, and where is that?'

'He's on the dole, dearest one. I hear he's doing *ever so* well.'

'Gosh, that's harsh.'

'It's a harsh industry, Kevin. It's a harsh life. And a very busy one. What do you want?'

'Ermm... I was wondering if I could have my old job back.'

There was a pause. Kevin just knew she was leaning back and crossing her legs. He could see the coffee cup on the desk with the rich pink impasto lipstick around the rim.

'Were you, indeed? Literary editor, weren't you? Bit of an old-fashioned job. I plan for this paper to be a bit more forward thinking, darling. The Globe will have more of a presence in the twenty-first century.'

'Erm...Is there anything?'

'Well, there might be. There might be. It depends. What do you think you could offer the Globe, Kevin?'

It was a good question. He really ought to have expected it and had an answer ready. He began to worry that there was no answer. At least not that would get him any employment. He decided to remind her that he had a sense of humour. That can come in handy in some newspaper jobs.

'Well, I don't really want to be the Kazakhstan correspondent.'

'Oh no, indeed. If we took you back, honeybunch, I'd want you right here where I can see you. And I think I know exactly what you can do.'

Kevin was amazed when she offered him a job. The money would barely allow him to achieve parity with the Big Issue sellers, but it was a job. He was a bit puzzled though. After all, she had always disliked him. Perhaps she didn't bear grudges. Or perhaps if you don't like someone, what better revenge than to have him as an underling? He decided to give her the benefit of the doubt.

'Sounds great, Sarah,' he said weakly. 'I can't wait to come back.'

On Monday, he started as the Globe's new television critic. This had once been an influential and enviable post but had lost some of its glamour, as terrestrial television was less important these days, especially to young people, who watched strange and esoteric things on their telephones and tablets. Still, he could not complain. And, as he was able to work four out of five days from home, he wouldn't even have to run into Sarah too much. This was a particularly salutary perk, since he was becoming more and more estranged from the world, which had bitten his supplicant hand so many times.

One day, he sat in front of his laptop at home, reading what he had written to himself:

Dancing on Ice was a bit of a disappointment this week: nobody fell over.

No, he couldn't start there. That was a sign-off line. He looked at his notes and began again.

The possibility of time dilation is a fascinating study. Whenever I watch Dr Who, its half-hour duration seems to spin out to an eternity. But that is nothing compared with the morbid longevity of the series itself. It seems to have outstayed its welcome by several aeons. Sometimes, like a cosmic pestilence, it goes away. But then it rises from the earth like the Silurian menace, to make an unwanted recrudescence, just when we hoped we have seen the last of it…

No, too cynical. He tried again.

The Daleks have made a welcome return to Dr. Who. One day – let's hope it isn't too far away – they may make a full end of him. So far, the doctor has prevailed against them every time, but they keep coming back. We must console ourselves with the thought that they only have to win once.

No, that wouldn't do. He began once more. But not with any great optimism. He knew what the problem was. A television critic, no matter how caustic and cynical, has to like television. He hated it. He hated every second of it. He wondered, in fleeting moments of paranoia, if Sarah had known that. He tried again.

Ah! Love Island! It reminds me of those carefree, halcyon days of my youth. The days when I didn't have to watch television for a living.

He affected to find that very funny. He started giggling. He couldn't stop giggling. Then he started to cry. He couldn't stop crying. When the cleaning lady let herself into his house, over an hour later, she found him sitting at the table, sobbing and giggling over his computer.

CHAPTER TWENTY-FIVE

Kevin put the last piece of Sellotape in place and leaned back to admire his handiwork. His Spy Detector was ready. It was a vast improvement on the old Ziegen-Wirbelsaule model, as it could tell you which spy service the suspect worked for. Not that he did not appreciate Theo's trailblazing work. But Kevin's updated version was made of baked bean boxes, which allowed for a more flexible design. Also, it had a special device incorporated, developed from an old doorbell, which told you if you were being followed.

He decided to take the device down to Pimlico for a trial run. It had a special telephoto lens attachment, made out of an old kaleidoscope he had found in the attic. You could aim it at MI6 from across the river. He reached over to a pile of business cards and put some in his pocket, just in case anyone stopped him.

KEVIN TREGENNIS
Freelance National Security Advisor and Analyst
Import Export
PO Box 150
0782 5674031

But first, he had to prepare himself. He did not go out much these days and always kept the curtains closed. This was a crucial security precaution. But to venture out into the hostile world, he needed an extra disguise. He opened the drawer of his desk and took out a false beard and dark glasses. He put on the false beard so that it completely

189

covered his real one. Then, turning his mac inside-out so that the tartan lining could be seen, he opened the door and ventured out into the night.

Meanwhile, a long way away, the Bavarian authorities were very concerned to hear that the old mine in the mountains had been broken into. With characteristic Teutonic efficiency, they organised a safety inspection party to go and investigate.

A three-man team drove up as far as the roads allowed and then walked the rest of the way. Properly equipped with lights and ropes, they made their way down into the bowels of the cave in order to ensure that no-one was trapped there.

They moved cautiously down to where the landfall had crushed poor Theo. They saw him sticking out from under a pile of rocks. Clearly, he had been there for a while. His body was not in a fragrant state. They searched his clothes but failed to find any identification papers in his pockets or amongst his bizarre set of belongings. The dead man seemed to have brought everything unnecessary for a day's underground exploring but nothing that might be considered necessary. There was a large amount of food but no means of opening or preparing it. Perhaps his pots and pans had been buried under the rocks. One of the party suggested that he might be English, and the others nodded as if this explained a multitude of eccentricities and contradictions.

One of the crew went up to call an ambulance as there was no signal below. The other two began to move the rocks in preparation to have the victim's body sent back to town. Eventually, they had moved enough stone to discover a silver flask in the left hand of the dead man. The top

190

of the flask was slightly loose so one of the searchers opened it. He sniffed it and then poured the liquid on the ground.

'Ochsenschwanzsuppe?' he exclaimed. Oxtail soup.

An interesting mystery, they thought.

Even further away, in Astana, Natalya Markeva lovingly polished her mantelpiece and then replaced all her treasured and devotional items. Although many Kazakhstanis were Muslims, she and her family came from transplanted Orthodox Russian Christians. Back in the old days of the Soviet Union, when Marxism was the controlling orthodoxy, it had been easier to be a Christian down here than in the Russian part. On both sides of the shelf, she replaced the icons of the saints that she prayed to most often. To one side was a photograph of Patriarch Kirill of Moscow, supreme head of the orthodox church - and to the other a photo of Vladimir Putin. Then the two giant scented candles in their ornate holders. Then the large ornate cross which had been in the family for decades. And finally in pride of place in the middle, she set the beautiful silver flask which she had found in a doorway early one morning on her way to her cleaning job in the city.

She had not opened it yet. Nor would she. Her children had strict instructions that when she died, her ashes were to be placed inside it. What luck to find such a pretty object - and it was just the job. A gift from providence for her piety. Of course, she was only fifty now and in excellent health. There would be, she hoped, many years to go before that eventuality. Death, she thought, as so many people thought, was a very long way off.

L - #0140 - 290923 - C0 - 210/148/11 - PB - DID3713277